MW01199204

The

Perv

Also by Rabih Alameddine

KOOLAIDS

Rabih Alameddine

Stories

The

Perv

Picador USA

Picador® is a U.S. registered trademark and is used by St. Martin's Press under license from Pan Books Limited.

Book design by Gretchen Achilles

Library of Congress Cataloging-in-Publication Data

Alameddine, Rabih.
    The perv : stories / by Rabih Alameddine.—1st Picador USA ed.
      p. cm.
    Contents: The perv—The changing room—Duck—My grandmother, the grandmother—Whore—Grace—A flight to Paris—Remembering Nasser.
    ISBN 0-312-20041-2 (hardcover)
    1. Lebanon—Emigration and immigration—Fiction.
2. Lebanese—Foreign countries Fiction. 3. Lebanese Americans Fiction.
    I. Title.
PS3551.L215P47   1999
813'.54—dc21
                                    99-25993
                                    CIP

FIRST EDITION: JULY 1999

10 9 8 7 6 5 4 3 2 1

For Randa, who stands by me

For Rania,

Light of the world,

Queen of the universe,

Beloved by all,

Our true Aphrodite

For Raya

Acknowledgments

I have been blessed with a number of friends who read my work critically. My thanks to Asa DeMatteo, William Zimmerman, and Gretchen Schields. I would not have been able to write without the support and hospitality of Dan Read, Andrea Laguni, Tom Brady, Flavio Frontini, Carlo Togni, Robert Riger, Michael Davis, Dana Gallo, Paul Bartel, Amy Tan, Norman Laurila, and Sami Abdel-Malak. I gratefully acknowledge my teacher Brugh Joy.

I thank my editor, Michael Denneny, and at Picador/St. Martin's, George Witte, Robert Cloud, Sarah Rutigliano, and Linda McFall.

I wish to acknowledge the existence of The One Who Shall Remain Nameless.

I have always thought that a writer is as original as the obscurity of his sources. My sources have never been obscure. Many writers have influenced my work, but for one story in particular, I have to mention Patrick White's *The Vivisector. Whore* could not have been written without it.

Contents

The

Perv

The Perv

Wanted:Teen Son/Friend
You're 18 max., honest, caring, athletic, good kid. Very slim, hairless build. Extremely young boyish good looks/cute. I am honest, caring, adventurous, good person, 6'1", 205. My interests include all sports, fitness, travel, outdoors, photos, painting, warm times, teen boys, fun, languages ++. Bill—Box 16, 420 NW Ninth Ave., Portland, OR 97209

Sammy has the perfect name for a young boy. It works on a number of levels. One first notices the androgynous nature of the name. It appeals to a larger number of people than a more common androgenic name like Tom, John, or George. In any case, none of these names would have worked, for Sammy is Lebanese. It is one of the few names that is both Arabic and Western. Even the pronunciation is almost the same. *Sammy* in Lebanese would have a little bit of a longer *a* like *Sam* in English, so it would be like *Sam* with a *y*. His parents would not have been able to give him a Western name without identifying him as Christian. Sammy is a name used by both Christian and Muslim Lebanese. So, you see, the boy has the perfect name.

I know you think of me as a pervert. You judge me. By your standards, I am a pervert. But who are you to judge? What gives you the right to decide what I do is perverted? What makes you think you know what is moral? Is your life so pure? I doubt it. What did Jesus say about throwing the first stone? Yet all you followers of Jesus judge the most harshly. You are so stuck in your ways. You believe you know what is right and what is wrong, what is moral and what is immoral. You think you have the right to judge. That is so unfair.

If I am a pervert, it is God who made me this way.

I am tired. I do not wish to convince you of anything. If you want to judge me, go ahead. You can read this or not. I do not give a damn anymore. I've given up. You go ahead. Think what you will.

Dear Bill,

Hello. My name is Sammy. I am responding to your ad in *Boyheaven*. I am hoping you could be my pen pal. I am looking for gay men to get to know. I live in the San Francisco Bay Area. We just moved here two years ago. I am from Lebanon.

You can write me at my uncle's address. He's gay and lives in San Francisco. But please don't write anything funny on the envelope. OK? I told him I am looking for a pen pal, but I didn't tell him where I got the ad from.

Anyway, my interests include sports too. I like all sports, but particularly soccer. I play about four times a week. I will be starting high school in September, and I was told I would probably be able to make the school team unless lots of good players come in at the same time. I like going to movies a lot. I like reading. I read everything. I also like computers a lot. I am writing this letter on a computer.

Anyway, I have to go now. I hope you can write me back soon. Tell me about yourself and everything.

Sammy

Sammy really is a nice boy. He is well behaved. Like most boys his age, he is very confused about his sexuality. Then again, he believes he is gay. He is attracted to men sexually. That seems to be a given.

He thinks he has been gay for as long as he can remember. His earliest memories always included an attraction to men. That much is known. He is not that confused about his sexuality after all. Unlike other boys his age who could be confused, Sammy is not. That is what makes him special, and a little different.

I'm getting old. Old, old, old, old. I hate it. You may have guessed it. Today is my birthday. I never liked birthdays. Not mine or anybody else's. We make such a big deal out of them. One year closer to death. I really hate it. I need a breather. I need to figure things out. I wish time would just stand still for a while and let me catch up.

I do not know whether the lack of energy I am experiencing is due to my disease or my aging. Does it matter? Why do I worry about such things? Either way, my body is decaying. Isn't that a wonderful thought? I am decaying. Well, my body is. My mind remains active, if a bit more cynical. I am old and I hate it. Where have all those years gone? I wonder if other people are as obsessed about growing old as I am. I mean, I do know that everybody is concerned about growing old, but are they as obsessed about it? Are you?

Hi Sammy,

I just received your letter and wanted to reply to you right away. We have so many things in common. My favorite sport is also soccer, or what the rest of the world calls football. I both coach and play the game. I coach the high school junior varsity soccer team. I've been coaching for 12 years. We finished 10-1-5 and tied for second place. I play on a team in the men's league.

I like to participate in all kinds of sports: tennis (I play that the most), handball and racquetball (helps me keep in shape), basketball, and I also snow and water ski. My other interests include world travel, languages (Spanish, French, Romanian, and a little German, Portuguese, Italian, and Vietnamese), black-and-white photography, fitness (weight lifting), outdoor, camping, adventure, young boys!!!, reading, movies, the arts, etc.

I love life and I like trying new things. Unfortunately, I don't have a computer yet, but I am thinking of getting one. What would you recommend? I would be interested in knowing what you think.

For 18 years I lived in Tulsa. When I finished high school, I went to college in New York. Then I taught Spanish in high school in California (Modesto), Chicago, and finally Portland. I like teaching and coaching. I coached the boys' teams in baseball, basketball, tennis, soccer, and American football.

I played on teams in all those sports in college and high school as well. I always loved sports. Don't you?

When I came to Portland and the Northwest, I really liked mountains, lakes, oceans, desert, river—nature. So I stayed.

Now I have a contracting business and build and renovate homes.

This year two boys, really great kids from Romania, are living with me and going to high school. They are brothers and straight, I think (I know they are brothers, I think they are straight, ha ha!). For Christmas we went to Texas for three weeks. We drove through Oregon and California a couple of weeks ago. Reached as far south as Carmel and Monterey. We stayed in San Francisco for a day also, which was too bad because I didn't know you then or we could have met and gotten to know each other.

Since I love to travel and love being in different cultures, I have lived around the world. I've lived and traveled in Vietnam, Australia and New Zealand, Brazil, Colombia, Equador, Costa Rica, Nicaragua, Guatemala, Mexico, most of Europe (East and West). I lived in France and Germany for a year. Taught English in Germany and coached basketball and tennis in France. From '92–'94 I lived in Romania, where I taught English, PE, and coached sports. I also played on soccer and basketball teams there.

I'd like to get to know you, Sammy, find out about the things you like. What do you study in school? What classes are you taking? What are you favorite subjects? How long have you known you liked men and when did you find out? Do you know any young gay boys your age?

Feel free to ask me anything you want.

Would you please send a couple of photos of yourself? I would love to see what you look like.

Write soon.

Bill Wesselman

Box 16, 420 NW Ninth Ave., Portland, OR 97209

Sammy looks really sweet. He seems to have light blue eyes and dark brown hair, which is a little curly, giving him a somewhat angelic look, as if he has a halo. The hair looks slightly unmanageable, an impish quality, further emphasized by a mischievous smile. He is not necessarily handsome, but definitely cute. He'll be a cutie-pie for a long time to come, and when he gets older, he will probably be better than average. He seems to be on the small side, probably no more than five feet five inches, maybe a hundred and fifteen, but who can really tell from a tiny black-and-white photo?

You can tell some things from a picture. You can tell that Sammy is really adorable. You can tell he is innocent, looking forward to life. His picture shows him smiling. A lovely smile. It shows a boy at the age before life has begun to oppress. Everything is possible. Nothing is out of his grasp. Sammy is a boy with a lot of potential.

I wonder sometimes if I need help. I swear to you, I have been to therapists and psychiatrists. Nothing worked. I have tried many different therapies to no avail. I have been on many medications. A miracle drug, they told me. I believed them at one point. I took so many. I don't recall the names anymore as much as I recall the colors. Blue pills, red pills, yellow-striped pills. I had all kinds. I took antidepressants. You'd think that would work, wouldn't you? No. Nothing worked.

I know what you're thinking. I really do. You're thinking castration. Hell, California's glorious governor, the evil Pete Wilson, signed a bill, didn't he? Do you think that would work? You're fooling yourselves because my problems have nothing to do with my balls. Not a single thing. But I know you fucking jump to conclusions. You ought to be ashamed of yourselves.

Did you ever stop to think that you are the perverts, not me?

Dear Bill,

I just got your letter. It was great. I think you were reading my mind. My uncle asked me if I got a picture of you so I showed him the one with Nicolae and Tomas and I told him Tomas was you. See, he keeps after me to find a boyfriend my age so I had told him, you, my pen pal, were around my age. I couldn't believe how lucky that you sent that picture. This must be fate or karma or something like that. It must be. How else would it have happened so great?

The pictures are great. When I first saw them, all I

could say was WOW! Boy, you sure are handsome. You really are. Really cute. When I saw your ad, I wrote but I was expecting the worst. Not that it really mattered since we're only pen pals and I would have written to you anyway, no matter what you looked like. But it was great to find out you're so cute. How old are you anyway? You have a nice house and your boat is great. Do you water-ski a lot? I don't do it as much, but I love it. We water-ski in the Delta over here. I was very happy to hear about you coaching soccer. That's my favorite sport. I love it so much. I play all the time.

I didn't know you were in Bucharest. Well, come to think about it, I didn't know anything about you! I was there too. We went on vacation there. I don't remember much. I think my father had business in Romania.

You asked me how long I have been gay. I think I have been as long as I remember. Not that anyone can tell. I don't look gay or anything like that. Even my uncle didn't know until I told him, but his boyfriend said he knew I was, but I think he just said that because I told him nobody could tell. My uncle is a nice guy and I really like him, but he is silly sometimes. He thinks I am too young to worry about being gay and stuff like that, but I think he is worried that my parents would be upset with him, which is really silly. He doesn't want me to tell any of his friends that I am gay, which is also silly. I like him anyway. I also like his lover, who is really cool. I like visiting them a lot because they live in San Francisco, near the Castro, which is a lot more fun than where I live. Anywhere is more fun than where I live.

I don't have a boyfriend yet. The only guy I fooled around with is my brother. You can't tell anybody that, okay? He would get really upset if I tell anybody. He is straight though. He's 17 and he is having sex with his girlfriend so we don't fool around as much anymore so I'm looking for a boyfriend because I think about it all the time. Do you have a boyfriend? How old is he? You said you are interested in young boys!!! I thought that was funny (the exclamations). Well I like men!!! but I don't know whether men would be interested in me. My uncle says that a lot of men would be, but that I should find a boyfriend my age. I don't care as long as he is a nice guy.

You asked me what I am studying in school. I will be starting high school in September. I will be studying the usual stuff. I will be attending Lowell High School, which is a magnet school. I will be going there because they have a great math program and I am very good at it. I have already started calculus, which is why Lowell has recruited me. I am a very good student, but I don't think I am as good as everybody thinks I am. I just look good because most students here in America don't study like we used to. I find it surprising how bad most kids are in math over here. Lowell High School is going to be interesting. All the kids are smarter than anywhere else. That should be interesting. But I have already been told that I will be the only one taking the math classes, which means that there is no one else who is as good as I am, which is not so good. Anyway, since all the kids are smart, the soccer team is not the best, which means I will probably be able to make the varsity or the junior varsity at least, which should be fun.

High school is going to be interesting. I think I can make lots of friends. Most of the people at Lowell are Chinese. I hope I can get along with them. I don't have any gay friends. I am hoping that maybe when I get to high school,

I will be able to find some. I don't know how yet, because I can't tell who is gay and who isn't. And if somebody is really gay, then I don't really like them, like if they act like girls or stuff like that.

I will be traveling to Europe soon. Sometime in early June. I leave with my folks, so that should be fun. You should write me again soon, before I leave. Okay?

Questions for you. Okay? Do you have a boyfriend? When you said you like young boys, does that mean you like them as boyfriends? Does that mean you don't have friends your age? Do you have a boyfriend your age? Do you like sex with young boys or with men? You're not married, are you? Do you have lots of gay friends in Portland?

Anyway, I hope you like my picture. I don't have many pictures because they make me look dorky. Mom says I don't look dorky, but I still think I do. But anyway, the picture should give you an idea what I look like but I look better in person!

Is your name Wesselman? I couldn't tell from the handwriting so excuse me if I wrote it wrong. Does that mean you are Jewish? If so, have you ever been to Israel? I haven't, but would like to someday. It's the closest country to Lebanon, but I have never been there.

Anyway, please write soon. I can't wait to hear from you. And you can feel free to ask me anything you want too.

Sammy

Sammy is so full of life, gregarious. Life seems to have blessed him. Everybody loves Sammy. He seems to have it together. People like to be around a boy with such a wonderful attitude. He inspires those around him. He is just one of those people that other people want to hold and hug and play with.

He moved to the United States from Lebanon a couple of years ago. It could not have happened at a better time. It could not have happened to a better boy. Can you imagine the kind of pressure he must have been under growing up in a war-torn country? Can you imagine the kind of tragedies he must have suffered? No, you cannot fathom that angelic face going through horrific experiences. You would want to save him. Yes, that face would demand it of you. Lebanon does not deserve Sammy. No, he was born to become an American. America needs boys like him.

Vigor, that's a better word. Sammy is full of vigor.

I woke up today with a pain in my side. It is a dull, constant pain, not throbbing or stabbing. It is on my right side, a little under my liver. I always try to document the type and location of my pain. It makes it more real. Without that, people would not believe me, and if they do not, then they say I am hallucinating or faking it. My pain is real, believe me.

I don't know where the pain came from. I don't think it was because of the way I slept. Every day it is something new. Ah, fuck. Fuck, fuck, fuck, fuck. I bet you it will get worse before the end of the day.

I, like Thomas Jefferson, believe the art of life is the art of avoiding pain. I do not understand some philosophers' infatuation with the idea of pain. Slow, protracted pain that takes its time and in which we are, as it were, burned with green wood does not improve me, or deepen me for that matter. It *hurts* me. Philosophers are so full of it.

I would give anything for a day without some kind of pain. I have not had one since I was a boy. Those were the days. Not just happy days, but pain free. Why do those days seem like such a distant memory?

Hi Sammy,

I was so happy to get a letter from you. I think we have some kind of karma between us already. It was strange because this morning I had a feeling that a letter from you had arrived at the place where I get my mail. Even though I had gone there yesterday to pick up the mail, I went again today and guess what? Your letter was the only one there. We must be on the same wavelength. Isn't that great?

I was very surprised you thought I was cute. Not many people do, but thanks. Now you, I can say, are very cute. I'll tell you how old I am in the next letter. But before I do that, I want you to take a wild guess when you write next. How old do you think I am?

I play soccer once a week. What about you? How often do you play? And what position? I'm usually center midfielder, but sometimes if my team needs to score, I move up and play forward. Last week we played a terrible game and we couldn't score at all, so this week I played up front. I scored once and got an assist and we won 2–1. I liked it much better this week. We also go out waterskiing 2–3 times a week during the summer. A lot of Romanian boys stay with me during the summer and the rest of the year and they have never skied before. So I take them out on my boat whenever I can because it makes them happy.

How long were you in Bucharest? When? How did you like it?

Does your brother know you're gay?

I am not married now nor have I ever been. And I don't have a boyfriend either. I have many friends, gay, straight, or whatever. We play sports and do a lot of fun things together like go out to dinner and movies. I like people of all kinds, but sexually I am only attracted to young boys like you. I don't find men sexually or physically attractive at all. You asked about young boys. I like them as friends or also in a father-son type relationship. I had a boy move in with me when he was 14. We stayed together until he joined the navy at 16. Those three years we did everything together—travel, work, play, grow, etc. I loved him and vice versa, which was really wonderful. I want to share my entire life with the right boy.

It sounds like you really got the high school figured out. Is the school a private school? Are you an Einstein in math?

Your photo was nice. Do you have a Polaroid? I'd sure like to see a photo of you in a swimsuit (or out of a swimsuit). Would you feel comfortable with that?

My name is from my German side (I'm not Jewish). My mother's side is Romanian.

I've never been to Israel. What do you think of Israel? Are you pro Israel, against it, or neutral? Are you Muslim or Christian?

Are things much better in Lebanon now? Do you and your family want to go back to live? To visit?

Where will you go in Europe? When? How long? Have you traveled in Europe before?

There's a good chance I'll go there for a couple of months also. When I lived in Bucharest for 2 years, I bought a used VW in Germany that I used. I left it in Romania with a friend. Nicolae and Tomas go back on June 25th. I may go then, get the car, and travel through Ireland and Scotland. Or I may go to some of the Italian, French, and Spanish beaches. There are some really cute young boys there—almost as cute as you!

You said to ask you anything. Ready?

If you were with a nice man, what sort of things would you like to do? Sexually, what do you think you would enjoy the most? Doesn't your uncle want to have sex with you?

Can you see what you can do about coming up with a few photos of the WHOLE you. You said that you have a really slim and hairless body; that really turns me on. Boys about your age who are totally hairless are the most attractive for me.

Write soon, Sammy—and send a few good (better) photos please.

Take care.

Love,

Bill

Box 16, 420 NW Ninth Ave., Portland, OR 97209

P.S. You said you mess around with your brother. What sort of things do you do? What did you like the most?

Sammy is brilliant. That is apparent to anyone who comes into contact with him. All you have to do is exchange a couple of words with him and you can sense that. He is precocious. A wonderful boy. His teachers obviously love him. It isn't every day that a teacher comes across a boy as charming, as intelligent, and as personable as Sammy. Most teachers spend a lifetime without coming across a boy like that. What a shame. That's what I say, what a shame. His teachers salivate at the mere idea of a boy like Sammy coming into their class.

What about his peers? Good question. There, he may have a problem. Since he is so intelligent, he really has nothing in common with his cohorts. He is ahead in his class so he does not come across boys his age much anyway. Most of his classmates are older boys and they would have little to do with him of course. Jealousy plays a part in his relationships with his peers. In fact, he is not well liked by the other kids. Boys his age can be so unkind and so, so cruel. They can tease mercilessly, play malicious games, or simply act savagely. They try to humiliate the boys that are different, especially those that are better than them. It is the way of life, the unfairness of it. This may explain why he gets along so much better with adults. They appreciate him more.

Sammy is a rarity, an incredibly smart boy who is not cocky, a boy who is down-to-earth, lovable, and incredibly cheerful. He still has not grasped how special he is, which, of course, makes him all the more special. A delightful peach.

I was once a boy with a lot of potential. At one point, I was destined for greatness. Destiny then proceeded to screw me. Fuck up my life, it did. What happened?

What happened to my life? I graduated from the best schools on three different continents. I never had a problem with studying. I had a natural ability when it came to being tested. I certainly had an above average IQ. I graduated everywhere with honors. I even got a graduate degree from Yale, a master's in sociology. They say one meets contacts in a school like Yale. All the movers and shakers of the world start there. I did not meet any of them. We must have hung out in different circles. I cannot figure it out for the life of me.

There were so many things that I was capable of, so many things I could have been or done. My potentialities were limitless. How could I possibly have fulfilled them? I started my own business. I did well, but never exceptionally so. It was never my fault. I was not a failure by any means. I accomplished what I set out to do, but I never received any breaks. Opportunity never really came knocking. Not even once, as I recall. It probably came to my door, looked in, and said, "This boy is doing okay, I'll go help someone else."

I never had a relationship. Never. Could you believe it? Well, you probably would, you assholes. You probably think I don't deserve to be in a relationship. Well, I do. It's just bad luck. I never found someone to love me. But don't think for a minute that I spent my time bemoaning that fact. I just went on with my life. It just did not amount to much. That's all. And it isn't that it did not amount to much objectively. It did not amount to much relative to all the potential I was supposed to have, relative to the sublime life I should have lived. Well, I know you're snickering, so fuck you. You can stop reading this anytime, you fucking jerks. Think about this before you do though: Are you happy? Are you satisfied with where your life ended up? Are you really, or are you deluding yourself again? Why do you think you are better than I am? Why? Go on, go fuck yourselves.

Dear Bill,

We sure are on the same wavelength. I am not surprised you had a feeling that my letter arrived. Things like that happen to me all the time. So I am not surprised. I am surprised you say that not many people think you're cute. I think you are very handsome. Really. You also have a great body, great muscles and all that. I think you're very attractive. Anyway, I don't think I am very cute. Everybody says I am, but it's not really true. Well, maybe cute, but not really handsome. I look dorky. But, I feel better about how I look these days anyway, 'cause all my uncle's friends say I am very cute, but none of the girls at school think I am, but since I am not as interested in what the girls think anyway, I feel better. Also Mom thinks I am very cute, but she doesn't count. I'll try to find some more pictures. I don't have any really. I always hated pictures and Mom keeps pestering me about taking pictures, but I won't let her. So I have to find someone else to take pictures of me because my mom might get suspicious. I'll try seeing if I can send one with a swimsuit. Your picture waterskiing was really great and guess where I was looking! I don't have a Polaroid. Maybe I can get my uncle to take pictures of me, but I am not sure he would be willing to take one of me without a swimsuit. Anyway, I know you say you like a slim and totally hairless body, but I really am hairless. I don't have any hair yet, not even down there, so I am not sure you would like a picture of me without a swimsuit. I am also not very big down there either. I am also not circumcised. So I'm not sure you would like it. But if I turn around, I have a great butt because I run so much. I'm proud of my butt and legs. Would it be too much to ask you to send me pictures of you without a shirt and without a swimsuit? I really would love that. But if it is a problem, don't worry about it, okay?

Let's see. To answer your questions about soccer. I too play center midfielder most of the time. Although now, since I play on teams where everybody is much older, I usually play left- or right-wing midfielder 'cause I am fast, but not big enough or strong enough to play center midfielder. I'm not yet 5'5", you see. I'm also two years younger than the next youngest guy on the team I play on. It will probably be the same thing in high school.

To answer your Bucharest questions. We were there for two weeks. That was a long, long time ago. I am not sure when it was. I don't remember much of it though. I was very young. My parents loved it, and they intend to go back. My dad has been there a couple of times without me.

How come you don't have a boyfriend or a lover? I want one. I am glad you are attracted to young boys sexually 'cause I am attracted to men I think.

Am I an Einstein in math? I don't think so, but everybody else seems to think so. I don't think I am an Einstein, I think they are not very good, that's all. But I am also good in English, and I draw and paint very well too. Lowell High is a public school. It is the best school in the area, public or private. It's a magnet school.

What do I think of Israel? The Israelis are okay. They can be assholes sometimes, but the same could be said of the Lebanese. I wish they would leave Lebanon alone. I still would like to visit sometimes. I am Christian, which is why I am not circumcised. Things are better in Lebanon. But no, I will not go back. I already told my parents that I like it much better over here. I would stay with my uncle if they decide to go back. I like it much better over here. And the men are much cuter!

What do you mean by father-son relationship? I am not sure about that. The magazine *Boyheaven* said that a lot, but I was never sure what it means. I just thought it meant sex between a dad and his son, which is not going to happen in my case 'cause my dad would freak out royally.

We will probably start in Paris. After that I am not sure. Probably to the south of France for a while. We should be back by mid-July. We lived in Paris before we came here. I love the city but not the French. French men are ugly anyway and they smell.

Now to answer your difficult questions. But you can't tell this to anyone, okay? You have to promise not to tell anyone because I would be in trouble. If I was with a nice man, what would I like to do? I don't know how to answer that. I would probably say, whatever makes him happy. I like doing all sorts of things so anything would be good. I would love to go waterskiing and swimming (nude swimming would be best!). I like to go out to nice restaurants and go to movies. I would like to be with a nice man who would like me. That's important. I want a man who would like me and kiss me a lot. I want a man who would like me and want to hug me all the time. Hug me always and kiss me. I want a man who would hold me and cuddle and stuff like that, but they have to like me. I want a man who wants to touch me and kiss me all over and I want to kiss him all over. I want to lie back and have him kiss me all over the place. And I want him to lie back and let me do the same to him all the time. I want to be able to sleep on a man's chest and I want to kiss his butt (I know that's weird, but I want to do that). I want to be with a guy who likes to play with my butt (that's weird too). Anyway, my uncle doesn't want to have sex with me. He says I am way too young to have sex, which just shows you how silly he is. But his lover doesn't think so. I messed around with him. When I told him I have never had a blow job, he gave me one. He also kissed and licked me all over including my chest and he even put his tongue back there, in my butt and all. But he didn't let me do anything to him. With my brother we messed around a lot for a long time. I was much younger when he had me play with his thing. I used to do it all the time. Then he wanted me to suck him, which I learned how to do and we did that for a long time. I didn't like it at first but when his dick got bigger and he got a lot of hair, I really liked it better. I also liked kissing and licking his balls. That was my favorite. But the best, and you can't tell anybody this, is when he started to fuck me. That was the best. We never did it much because he thought it was weird that I liked it. But I did like it a lot. I like anything to do with my butt. Anyway, my brother says he didn't like fucking me because he likes girls. He says he is straight. I am not because I like getting fucked.

Anyway, I told you everything. Now it is your turn. Can you tell me what you like to do or what you would like to have done to you? And please don't tell anyone what I told you. Also could I have a picture of you without a swimsuit? Also if you like, you can send me your number and I can call you if you want. Anyway, that's it for now. I am going to mail your letter right now and then run into the bathroom to do you know what!

Write me soon, please. I like your letters a lot so please write soon.

Sammy

Sammy is a lucky boy. He has been sexually awakened at a fairly early age. He was initiated into rituals that will be of great help to him as he grows up. He is also smart and intuitive enough to understand many things that many boys twice his age have not begun to fathom. He understands what a real man can offer him. Beyond just simple pleasures, he understands the kind of sexual relationship and its concomitant ecstasies that a man can offer. That is a gift. Sammy is a gifted boy.

Since Sammy is now twelve, almost thirteen, he must have started fooling around with his brother when he was nine or so. Such a precocious child. Most boys his age have these unexplainable sexual urges. Sammy fulfills his. He also explains them well, quite eruditely I might add. Sammy is a gifted boy.

All boys his age are sweet, but Sammy is extrasweet. Other boys are just beginning to awaken to life. Sammy has not only awakened to life, but has already begun to swallow it whole. Sammy is definitely a gifted boy.

————

Another operation. I will be hospitalized for four weeks. The doctors seem pretty confident. I'm not. I am never confident. How can one be confident when it comes to an operation? The doctors call it minor surgery. As someone said, minor surgery is when they perform it on someone else. You open me up and it is not minor.

Four weeks away from the world. I have to stay in the hospital for the doctors to make sure everything is hunky-dory. Four weeks in a sterile hospital room. With my luck I will have a moaning, whining, snoring roommate. How could I stand it?

I will visualize myself in Europe. Nice beaches, south of France. It works sometimes. It will probably hurt. I will visualize a bad sunburn. I bet Bucharest is nice this time of year.

Hi Bill,

Yes, this is a second letter. I got so excited when I was writing you the other one that I forgot to guess your age. I really liked your letter and I was very happy so I wanted to send it out right away and then I forgot. Anyway, I think you are 35. You look much younger than my dad does and he is 44. But then you might be older because you asked me to guess and I figure only people who look younger ask people to guess. Am I right?

Anyway, I wish I were going to Europe with you and not my parents. You sound like a lot more fun. We don't do anything and they always watch everything I do so it gets boring. I even suggested that I should stay here with my uncle, but they didn't agree. Also my uncle doesn't want me to stay with him 'cause he worries so much. I go through his gay magazines and all that.

I was really happy you thought I was cute. I was worried when I sent you my picture because I am not as good-looking as Nicolae or Tomas. So it was great to know that you think I am cute. Your letter got me so excited. I even jerked off thinking about it. I hope you don't mind my telling you that. I jerk off a lot anyway. It's the best thing. I do it whenever I can.

Anyway, I hope to hear from you soon. So bye for now.
Sammy

Sammy's parents are not fun people. They are obviously not creative enough, or skilled enough. The boy needs to be intellectually entertained. His parents are not up to the task. They gave him birth, but that was about it. After that, they were unable to give him much. They are not up to the challenge of having such a brilliant progeny. A shame really. It happens often, more often than people realize. Too many young boys never reach their potential because their parents are too limited.

They were able to offer a worldview. That was not really planned on their part. They simply enjoyed traveling and they brought him along to save on baby-sitters. Sammy gained invaluable experience. In that at least, they were better than your garden-variety, run-of-the-mill American parents.

He needs something more.

I have considered suicide. I truly have. I get so depressed at times. What's the point? I am a Catholic. I may not practice these days, but it doesn't let go of you that easily. The Church is not an easy ex-mistress. Give me a boy until he is five, the priest would say, and I will give you a Catholic for life. I never attempted suicide though. I considered, went as far as planning it, but could never pull the trigger. I studied required dosages. I researched least painful methods. I even went through the entire process of registering and buying a gun. When it came time, I could not pull it off. It is a weakness of mine, you would say.

I have been depressed most of my life. I never seem to snap out of it. Nothing really helps. Prozac helped for about a month. I began to feel better for a little while. I started seeing colors for the first time. Then, bang, I was right back where I started. I tried Zoloft, and many more drugs whose names sound weirder, but were less effective. The depression never journeyed too far. Nobody has been able to figure out why. Just my lot in life, the hand I was dealt, so to speak.

Dear Bill,

You have not written in a long, long time, so I figure you're upset with me. I figured something like this was going to happen when I wrote all that stuff about sex. You must think I'm bad or something. I'm sorry. I guess you don't want to talk to me anymore. I figured this was going to happen when I saw how handsome you were. Anyway, I'm sorry this happened because you sounded like a really nice guy.

We leave for Europe tomorrow. If you were going to Bucharest, then we could have met there 'cause we are going there June 30th for a couple of days. I guess this means you don't want any more pictures from me.

It has been a really terrible couple of weeks. My cat, Trumpet, fell out the window and disappeared for one whole week. I spent the whole week looking for him but he was hiding because he was so afraid. He's not a year old. Then one night I found him hiding in the ivy. He was starving and he had two broken bones in his foot. So I took him to the vet and they put him in a cast but it is going to cost me $500. My dad says that I promised I would take care of him and pay for everything. So when I get back, I have to find a job that would be able to pay my dad back. Also one of my friends turned into a creep last week. So all in all I have been feeling awful, so I was kinda expecting something bad to happen with your letter.

Anyway, I'm sorry if you got upset with what I said in my letter. I knew it was going to happen. I had never told anybody all that and just wanted to tell someone. I'm sorry if it got you upset. Anyway, I guess it's hopeless 'cause everybody is upset with me these days. I hope you have a wonderful time on your trip. I'm really sorry I got you upset.

Bye.

Sammy

Sammy is an emotional boy. His hormones are raging, which affects his behavior. He does rash things, unable to explain them even to himself afterwards. He feels betrayed by adults. He must be protected. Sometimes, he gives the impression he is an adult because of his maturity and perspicacity, but of course he isn't. Sammy is only twelve, a precocious twelve, but twelve nonetheless. He does not have the emotional maturity one achieves with age, or the patience for that matter.

Sometimes he feels vulnerable. He looks really sweet when he is vulnerable. Cuddly and sweet. One wants to hold him and comfort him. It's okay, Sammy, things will be okay. You want to hold him and take care of him, make his problems disappear. Your heart hurts because you want to help.

I rarely see the sun anymore. The light hurts my eyes. I have adjusted to life without natural light. Heavy, floral curtains are my barriers. Whether to keep the light out, or my spirit in, is yet to be determined.

I have not ventured out of my room in about a year, except for hospital visits. The disease does not allow me. My world centers around this container. I still follow diurnal rhythms—for what reasons, I am not completely sure. I keep track of seasonal changes by variations in temperature.

I read less often these days. The words are much too small. They tire my eyes. That loss has been the most painful to adjust to, more racking than losing people close to me. Oprah and Ricki are my constant companions. My modem is my best friend.

Friends come over less and less often. I don't blame them. I am terrible company. I have daily visits from the home-care nurses. They deliver my food. They clean my room weekly. All my needs are taken care of.

But you still hate me.

Hi Sammy,

How are you doing?

You are a pretty smart cookie, Sam. I can't believe I'm writing a boy as smart as you are. You were so right about my age, which is why I think you are smart. I prefer to put it this way: I've had sixteen thirty-ninth birthdays. Now come on, get out your calculator and figure this out.

I wish you were going to Europe with me also. We'd have a great time together, you and I. I'm sure of it!

I took the boys, Nicolae and Tomas, on a trip to Victoria, Vancouver Island, where we stayed with friends for four days. We did a lot of hiking and camping. We water-skied. We played tennis and we had an all-around great time. I wish you could have been with us. That would be such fun.

When it comes to sex, I prefer a boy like you. T and N are a little older than I prefer and really too hairy. Don't get me wrong, I love both of them because they are really good kids, but physically I'm not attracted to them. You may not like being totally hairless, but that really turns me on. I don't like hair on boys at all.

I am happy with the boys living with me right now because we get along so well. The problem is that since they live with me, I cannot have a boyfriend right now. The kids and I are so busy together, we do so many exciting things (except sexual things) that I don't have time to look for a boyfriend. Also, since I only like cute young boys like you, I don't find them so easily. I meet boys here and there, but they don't always work out as boyfriends. I think it could work out between you and me if you were here, because we like to do the same things. I want to suck your hairless cock and balls, your thighs and butt. If you are really clean, I'd also like to suck your little butt hole and then fuck you like you want. I'd want you to fuck me too. Like you, I'd love to have you lie on top of me, cuddle, and feel all over your smooth, hard legs, butt, back, chest, etc.

Did he suck your nipples also? Of course I'd like to hug and kiss a cute boy like you also. Sure wish there was a way we could get together.

How far do you live from SF? How often do you go to your uncle's?

What I mean by a father-son relationship is finding one young boy who wants to be my son and I would be his father. I would do everything for him. I would treat him great. He would live with me and we'd do everything together, grow together, have fun together, and love one another deeply. I was in a father-son relationship with a boy once. He came to live with me when he was fourteen and he stayed for three years until he joined the navy. We loved each other very much and we had a wonderful relationship.

We did everything together, we traveled together, I took him many places, we played sports, we worked together, etc. I would like to find another boy like that. Someone who needs me and I need him.

You keep mentioning nude swimming. I fantasize taking you to a nude beach where we swim out until the water is above waist level; then, with everyone all around but unable to see, I dive under the water and slowly suck your cock and butt until you shoot off. Then you do the same to me.

In Bucharest, at the public pool I met one nice, cute boy. He was about 14 or 15; I swam past him. He was in the pool with his back against the wall. The first time I brushed against his skimpy swimsuit and he didn't move. The next time I swam past underwater (better view) I ran my hand up and down his cock. He pushed his hips toward me and got a hard-on. The next time I grabbed his cock, squeezed, and started jerking him off. When I came up for a breath, he said it felt good, so I lowered his Speedo, pulled out his cock, went underwater, and started to suck him. He got all glassy-eyed. Since a lot of people were in the pool, we decided to leave and go to my place, where we had a great time. Unfortunately he didn't live in Bucharest, he was only visiting.

How would you like to do something like that?

I don't have any nude or shirtless photos but I'll see what I can do.

Write soon and I hope you can send a few of those photos soon. Maybe your uncle's lover would take some nude photos. Be careful where you develop them. It would be best if you had a Polaroid.

Write soon.

Love,
Bill
Box 16, 420 NW Ninth Ave., Portland, OR 97209
PS. Does anyone else read these letters?

Sammy is a great boy, but let's face it, he's not getting what he really wants. Sammy is a great boy who wants a man to fuck him. He wants a man to take charge of him sexually and emotionally, someone who will help him along the way. He needs a man as a role model in his life, a man who is strong, intelligent, masculine, sincere, handsome, somewhat dominant, and nice. He wants a man to show him what it is like sexually. He wants a man who will love him completely and unconditionally, to possess him fully. Anyone can see that. Now he is actively searching. We can do a psychological analysis and find out why he wants a man to fuck him, but what good would that do? The boy is a good kid who knows what he wants. Let's just give it to him. All those in favor of Sammy getting what he wants, say aye. I.

Okay, I admit it. I'm not a very good person. I play with him. I play with his mind. It's the only entertainment left for me. I don't have much else left. I would be bored shitless otherwise. Do I plan to harm him in any way? No, I don't think so. You probably think that I have already done enough damage. I beg to differ. I'm just having a little fun here, nothing more. No harm done. It's not like I'm going to meet him. Really, think about it for a minute. You must think I am really stupid.

I get bored. I need to do something. Remember, after all, I was supposed to have all this potential. Do you know what kind of a curse that is? Do you? Well, I am very creative. What happens when a creative person has very few outlets for his creativity? He starts writing letters, I guess.

Hi Sammy,

I just received your letter and finished reading it. I thought I should write you quickly because you said you had not received a letter from me. That's really weird because I wrote you right after I got your letter. You don't have to worry about what you write to me. We're friends now and I want to know everything about you. Nothing you write will make me "MAD" or "UPSET." Be open and honest; that will *never* cause any problems between you and me.

The boys, Tomas and Nicolae, will be returning home to Romania on June 25th and I will leave here the next day to go visit my mom in Texas for a while. On July 4th I fly to Bucharest, where I'll visit everyone (I know so many people there) for a few days, and then I'll go get my 1984 VW that a friend has been using and keeping since I left. My friend tells me it is still running fine, so I hope it won't give me any trouble. Then I hope to go to Croatia, Slovenia, Bosnia, Italy, Austria, Switzerland. I might just stay someplace, however, if I think it's nice, so I don't really have any set plans.

I get back to Portland about Aug. 30th. I'll write to you then about the trip. Before then I would like to hear about your trip and what you did there. I hope you had a good time.

What will you do for the rest of the summer?

Let's keep writing, Sammy. As I said, you can always feel perfectly free to write to me about anything you like because we're friends and nothing you say will offend or hurt me. I want to know everything about you.

Write soon.

Love,

Bill
Box 16, 420 NW Ninth Ave., Portland, OR 97209

Sammy overreacts sometimes, but that is part of his charm. You just have to take it into consideration when dealing with him. He is passionate about everything. He is so full of energy, does life at full speed. Excitement is part of his being. He talks fast, reacts fast, and fucks fast. He hasn't fucked anyone yet, but when he does, he will do it fast. He will be so cute when he does it.

The nurse brought me some flowers today. I wonder why she keeps doing that. They do not last long in this room. Nothing does. She brought yellow roses. I hate yellow, always have. They stank up the room. She keeps saying flowers brighten up a room. It would take more than flowers for this job. At least this nurse does not talk as much as the Mexican one. Yack, yack, yack. How are we doing today? Are we comfortable today? No amount of silence would get her to stop. This nurse at least is semi-silent most of the time.

She changed the sheets. That was good.

Hi Sammy,

How are you? Hope you like my city—Bucharest! Too bad we don't meet. Bill give me you address. He say write—you good boy. Nicolae (my brother) and me returned on June 25th. It was great living with Bill in Portland. He is very good man. Good friend. Now he travels in Bosnia, Croatia, and Slovenia wants to see problems of war and help people. He lives with us (Mom and us two) when in Bucharest. He goes back to Portland on August 30.

Now we visit friend in country for three weeks. We start school first week of September. I will be in 10th grade again and Nicolae in 11th. Our Romanian school does not count our year in Portland. So must do it again here. That's okay. We learned much more than only school things—English, travel, and work with Bill was great. He paid us really good so now we have money for our college and things for Mom.

I write when we are back home. Nicolae and Bill say high also.

Tomas

It is incredible to notice how little effect the civil war in his homeland has had on this boy. He seems to be so well adjusted. Most people who experience a war become the walking dead. They shut down mentally and emotionally. Not our boy. He is so open to different experiences. He never protects himself, which is why he is in need of a man to take charge and provide guidance in his life. He needs a man to protect and take care of him. A man to allow him to blossom fully.

I get so bored in my room. I escape through fantasy. I live through metamorphosis. I can't help myself. I am very good at being anything other than me. People like me when I am someone else.

I once transmuted—I use the verb *transmute* because that is what happened; *transmute: to change from one form, substance, nature, state, into another*—to a fifteen-year-old, red-haired Brazilian boy. Irish ancestry to be exact. My father is German and my mom Irish, although she had lived in Rio most of her life. My name is Paolo. I stand five feet five inches, weigh around one hundred and fifteen pounds, have bright red hair and green eyes.

I have a slight accent. I am innocent, yet curious. I am ready to fall in love with an older male who wants to take care of me. Sometimes my father is understanding, sometimes he isn't. Sometimes I have a sexual liaison with my six-foot-two, blond, strapping father, and sometimes I do not. The story changes but I remain Paolo. Sometimes I have two older brothers who initiated me, along with my father, into man-to-man sex. Other times I am an only boy. I am an orphan whose parents were killed in a car accident, or I am living with a man because my parents were jailed because they embezzled large sums of money. I have achieved complete metamorphosis. Until it is time to move on.

Hi Bill,

It's now the end of August so I hope you're back. I was very happy to get your mail. I got two letters from you and I even got a card from Tomas. That was so great. It was wonderful. I'm sorry about the last letter I sent. I didn't receive a letter for a long time from you so I thought you were upset with me. I'm sorry. I should not have written that letter, but I was scared because I wrote so many things about sex and stuff. I got scared that you didn't like me anymore. Anyway, I am really happy that you like me. That's so great. It made me very happy and I'm not scared anymore.

I loved the card from Tomas. I wish I had gotten it earlier because I could have met him in Bucharest. We were there for a couple of days. Do you have his address? I should send him a thank-you note for the card and he didn't put his address down.

You asked me if anybody else reads these letters. No way. I hope nobody else reads my letters to you, or if someone does, then I hope you trust them not to tell anybody. I would be in big trouble if anybody reads the last letter I sent you. Okay? Please don't tell anybody about what I like for sex because I would get into trouble. And please don't tell anybody about my brother because he would get really mad. He's a jerk anyway and if he finds out I told anybody, he would get really upset. Nobody knows I am writing to you. My uncle thinks you are a pen pal who is my age and all we talk about is school stuff. I even told him that you said you like girls so he doesn't suspect anything. I think it is better if we left it this way because I could get in big trouble if anybody figured out what I am writing about.

I wish I had gone to Europe with you because I hate going anywhere with my family. All they want to do is boring stuff and I end up spending a lot of time on my own. My mom and dad leave my brother and me and go out and do what they want. Then my brother leaves me and goes and does his own thing so I end up spending most of my time alone. It sucks really. I didn't have a good time. I kept telling them I wanted to go back home and they said I was a whiner, which was not true because I was just bored. We spent some time at the beach in the south of France and that was okay because at least there when I was alone I was at the beach and I could do things, but otherwise it was really boring. Then my brother was really a jerk. He couldn't find a girlfriend so he started to fuck me again. But then he would get upset and he would call me names, but then he would fuck me again. I don't know what's the matter with him. So finally I got upset and told him I didn't want him to do it again. He then got really upset and called me all kinds of names. So I told him if he did it again, I would tell on him. So he got really upset and he has not spoken to me since. It's been four weeks and he has not talked to me. And everybody blames me. They all think I did something bad because they all think that he is such a great guy. My mom keeps saying that I must have done something really bad if he doesn't talk to me anymore.

Anyway, as if that's not enough problems, I had to work

all last month to pay the vet's bill for Trumpet breaking his leg. I made only $300, so now my dad says he is taking the rest out of my allowance. So I got into a fight with my dad yesterday. I think he is cheap. They pay everything for my brother, but when it comes to me, I have to pay for everything. I have to wear all his clothes. My bicycle is his old one, so is my tennis racquet, my soccer shoes, everything. They buy all the new stuff for him and I get it when he is done with it. And he is really stupid, you know. Really. He's four and a half years older than I am but only two classes ahead of me. But everybody thinks he's a genius. They all love him much more than me.

Anyway, I'm sorry about writing you all this but I am really mad right now. I wish you were here, then I could at least talk to you. But anyway, I'm all right now and school will start soon, so I will be getting busy and I will be away from my stupid brother and he will leave me alone.

Anyway, I was very happy that you said you liked me sexually. That really turned me on. I hope you don't get upset but I have been reading your letter a lot and I jerk off thinking about it. I would love to do all that and especially the thing at the nude beach under the water. I think you could do me, but I am not sure I would be able to do you because I would get too embarrassed with people around. Anyway, I love what you did with the boy in the pool. You are so lucky because you have tried a lot of things. I wish I could find someone to play with and do all those things myself. By the way, nobody has ever sucked my nipples but I play with them. I found out that if I play with them, they get really weird and they stand out. Well, the right one stands out more than the left one, and then when I wear a T-shirt you can see them, which is weird.

Well, I wish I were your son. I would love to do all those things with you. That would be really great and it would be a lot better than living here. I'm not sure what to do.

Anyway, I was also glad you said you like me hairless. I have good news for you and bad news for me! I still don't have hair. I now look with a magnifying glass every day and try to see when it is going to come out. I'm beginning to be afraid that it will never happen.

I better go now. I'll write you again soon. I hope to get a letter from you soon.

Bye now,
Sammy

Sammy can be so charmingly naive. He is a precocious, yet completely innocent boy. While in the south of France, he was on the beach alone—he spent most of the vacation alone, his uncaring and self-involved parents having other things to do—when he was approached by a middle-aged man. A homely man, he asked Sammy if he could take pictures of him. Sammy agreed even though he did not like the man, an American from Iowa. No, no, not an American. He was a German from Hamburg. Sammy tells the German that he would like copies of the pictures so he can send them to a friend, since he always thought of his friend during his monthlong vacation. The German asks Sammy if he would like to go up to his room before his wife gets back from shopping. They had a couple of hours before the wife returned. Sammy agreed. In the room, the German convinces Sammy to take his trunks off for better pictures. Sammy thinks it is great, for he can now send nude photographs to his good friend who wanted some badly. The German asks Sammy to jerk off for the camera. Sammy does so, giving his performance the same zest he gives everything. He finally ejaculates, and the man puts the camera away. Luckily the German did not touch

Sammy. No, no, the German came over and licked the semen off Sammy's groin area. Sammy, a little disgusted, but happy anyway for it is a small price to pay for getting those pictures to his friend, gives the German his address. The German promises to send him the photos.

Sammy is naive, but good-hearted. Of course the German never sent the photos. Sammy allowed a creep to photograph him jerking off, so he could send his good friend the pictures. Poor Sammy. He just wanted to make his friend happy and look what happened. One of these days he will begin to learn not to trust everybody, that not everybody is as kind and gentle as he. Until then, he'll just be our Sammy and we love him all the more for it.

It started out as a simple thing. I called one of those chat lines. I talked to this man. He asked me how old I was. I lied, telling him I was twenty-one. He did not believe me. I was embarrassed. I wanted to tell him my true age when he told me he did not mind that I was a minor. That took me by surprise. He insisted that I tell him my age. I offered eighteen. He did not believe me. I was younger. Sixteen, no. Not fifteen either. Finally I was thirteen, no pubic hair, slim, and cute as a button. He believed me. I was the horniest thirteen-year-old on the planet.

I logged onto America Online the first time as myself. Nobody would talk to me. Not a single person talked to me. I became Chester, a seventeen-year-old blond boy from Amagansett, New York. I was five foot nine, one hundred and fifty-five pounds, naturally toned (definitely not a gym bunny, though), with a nine-inch, uncircumcised penis. A high school senior and quarterback on the varsity team. Chester was basically straight, but about a month beforehand he was seduced by a friend of his father's on a fishing trip. Ever since then he had been thinking about sex with men. Well, every time Chester entered a chat room, everyone wanted to talk to him. Chester averaged one hundred and eighteen private messages a day. One hundred and eighteen messages a day; think about that for a minute. As myself, I never received a single message, other than junk mail from those who wanted to sell me pictures of naked men.

Is life unfair or what?

Hi Bill,

It's me. I'm writing you again because I think I sounded like a bad person in the last letter. Every time I write you I worry that you won't like me anymore. I told you that everybody was a jerk, which they are, but I am not a bad person really. I'm really a nice guy. My brother is the jerk, really he is. Nobody believes me because I am the younger brother and they all think I'm bad. I didn't want you to think I am bad too. I want you to really like me.

My brother is a jerk. I'll tell you what happened so you won't think I'm bad. You'll be the only one who knows. My brother hasn't fooled around with me in a long time. Every time we are alone together, he keeps calling me names. He calls me queer and faggot and all that. When we were in Europe, one night, all of a sudden, he comes over to my bed and puts his dick in my mouth and he starts pushing it in. Then he starts calling me a cocksucker while I am doing it and he keeps hitting me on the head and calling me names. I didn't say anything. The next night he does the same thing and then he fucks me. He knew I liked it, but he still just fucked me without even asking or anything. He kept calling me names too. He called me faggot and he even called me a slut, which is really stupid, since he is the only one who has fucked me, so how can I be a slut? He did on four different nights. Then one night, which was about five weeks ago, he was doing the same thing. He was fuck-

36

ing me and he called me a faggot and then he said I was going to get AIDS. I got really upset and started kicking him off me. He got upset but he didn't want to stop fucking me, but finally I kicked him off me and told him I don't want him to touch me anymore. He hit me. He hit me hard on the head. I told him if he touched me, I was going to tell on him. So he said he was not going to speak to me anymore.

Then my dad got upset with me because my brother was upset with me. Then my mom, who always takes his side, got upset with me. When I got fed up and told her he was a jerk, she slapped my face and told me never to say that about my brother. But he says that about me all the time. My dad is threatening to punish me if I don't make up with him, but I don't want to. So with all that, I was thinking of taking Trumpet and going away somewhere. I want to run away and never see any of my family ever again for as long as I live. I don't like them.

Anyway, I hope you don't think I'm not a nice boy because I am really. I just live with jerks.

Oh, and changing the subject, I saw your ad again in that magazine. Are you writing to other boys too? Are they nice? Are you going to have a boyfriend with one of them? How many are you talking to?

Also, does Tomas know you like boys? I want to write him back when you give me his address and I don't want to say anything that you don't want me to say. Again, I really wish I could have gone on vacation with you and not my folks. Maybe sometime we can get to talk. Well, I hope to hear from you. I hope this letter doesn't make you think I'm fucked up.

Bye now,
Sammy

Sammy is a nice boy, if a little misunderstood. Some of the words used to describe him are *precocious, perspicacious, adorable, charming, sweet, cute, smart, reliable, mature, responsible, attractive, handsome, lovely, sexy, naive, innocent.* Innocence is the predominant characteristic these days. Yes, that's it.

There is a reason innocence is the predominant characteristic. I have found that it is the most sexually appealing one. Think about it for a minute. The more virginal the boys were, the more exciting. But, there must be a balance. If a boy is a complete virgin, totally innocent so to speak, the predator may pull back. So a balance must be struck. Sammy is very innocent, but not completely so. He strikes the perfect balance. Men want him.

I do not sound like a thirteen-year-old, nor do I write like one. I never figured out why people believe so easily. But I enjoy being an innocent twelve-year-old. It's better than being who I am. I know. I know. I am a pervert, but we have already established that. Am I a liar? Sure. What's the harm? I ask you. Who am I hurting? I create this fantasy. It's my only life, really. I'm not kidding. It's the only life I have. Do I hurt the people I write to, or talk to by phone? Maybe a little, but I rarely promise I am going to meet them. Well, sometimes I do, but not always. I do lead them on a little, but that's because they really want to be led, honestly. It is not my fault if they create this expectation, this fantasy about me and my availability. They have a need and I fulfill it. I am very good at that.

You check it out and decide for yourself. Read the letters and then decide for yourself. Did I really lead them on? Okay, I know. Sammy is only one of my many characters, and he really isn't even one of my better ones. I never kept many records. But you should be able to judge anyway. Really, you decide. You read everything and then judge me. I give you permission.

Hi Sammy,

How are you? How was your summer? I was very disturbed when you wrote just before you left on vacation and said you didn't get my last letter, which I wrote to you. I thought maybe your uncle opened my letter to you and read it and then threw it away without showing it to you. Maybe he doesn't like me to write to you because I am so much older than you and like you said he wants you to find friends your age. That's why I sent the postcard and signed Tomas's name to make him think that this letter is from Tomas since I am sending it from Bucharest.

Sammy, I really like you. You sound like a bright boy and you sure are very cute. Don't think for a minute that I will stop writing to you. I want us to be friends for a long, long time, so don't worry, I will always write you.

I have been in Romania since July 5th. From the 12th to Aug. 14th I drove through Slovenia, Croatia, and Bosnia. I wanted to see what happened in the war and if there is any way that I can help in the future. I may sponsor a couple of kids to come study in Portland next year. We'll see how that goes. What has happened here is truly terrible. I was so sad to see all the horrible things that had happened. It's a big catastrophe. All the homes, machinery, factories, schools, hospitals, for hundreds of kilometers in Croatia and Bosnia were totally destroyed. Thousands of innocent people murdered. I bet it was like this in Lebanon. Am I right?

How did you like Romania? Bucharest? How long did you travel? Where? I really wish that we could have met here. We could have so much fun, you and I.

I'll be back in Portland August 30th. Three boys from Romania will come to study in Portland for the year and live at my place. Two are in 10th grade, one in 12th. Why don't you come study in Portland? Wouldn't that be wonderful? I'm just dreaming!

If you get this, and I sure hope you do, we must come up with another plan. If I write from Portland, your uncle will know that it is me and he will probably get upset and not give you the letter. Is there another address I can send the letters to that causes no problems? How can we work this out, Sammy?

If there is a problem, you can call me collect anytime. I'd really like to talk to you and we'd be better friends. Also don't be afraid to write anything you want or ask any questions at all. Nothing will be a problem with me. Write soon, Sammy. Don't forget to let me know if there is another place where I can send the letter.

Also, do you have any other photos of YOU? ALL OF YOU?

Love,

Bill

Box 16, 420 NW Ninth Ave., Portland, OR 97209

503-555-7678

Sammy has no friends. He lives a very lonely life. He is not a loner by any means. He is simply not surrounded by people who appreciate him. If he were, he would flourish. All he needs is to be with someone who is a match for him. He gets really bored. Yes, that's it. Sammy gets really bored. He needs to be challenged constantly. No, no, he needs to be loved. He needs to be cuddled, hugged, and loved. He needs someone to alleviate the pain of loneliness. Yes, Sammy is lonely and needs to be loved. He is not bored. It is by no means his fault.

One of my favorite characters was Peter. He was sixteen. He was from Sweden and had been living in the United States for only four weeks. His father was a nuclear physicist and worked for the Livermore Laboratories. Peter found it hard to adjust to life in an American city.

He lasted for about six months. It started out on the Internet. A doctor fell in love with him. The doctor was a thirty-seven-year-old general practitioner. I would have preferred a surgeon. They make more money. Peter and the doctor had a phone affair that lasted six months. The doctor was a gentleman. He stopped pressuring Peter to meet, once Peter promised that only the doctor would deflower him. Unfortunately for the doctor, Peter came up with some weird diseases. His mother took him on long trips. The soccer coach asked him not to have sex for a week. All in all, the doctor waited for six months, and then Peter got bored.

Hi Sammy,

How are you doing? I hope things are better with your family, but from your description of your brother it doesn't look good for you. Too bad he is that way. It sounds like the only one he is concerned with is himself. A very selfish person. You were right to tell him to stop or you'd tell your parents. Too bad you aren't living up here. I'm sure we'd have a great friendship.

I started playing soccer again last week with my team. The season has just started so I am not in as good of a shape as I should be. The legs felt pretty heavy after a while and I was very sore the following day. I'll be playing twice a week from now on.

This summer I was in Europe most of the time. I stayed at Tomas and Nicolae's house in Bucharest for ten days, then I drove through Bosnia and Croatia for a month.

It is a very sad situation in Bosnia and Croatia. Most of the homes are completely destroyed. Many of the Muslims were murdered. I guess it was a little similar to the way it was in Lebanon, eh?

When I returned here on August 30th, there were seven Romanian kids here living in my house. Now there are four. It's a little cramped since it is only a one-bedroom house. Three of them are in high school. Two sophomores and one senior. One was in senior year here two years ago and returned for six months. He works in construction with me now.

Sammy, is there any way I can contact you quickly if and when I go to the San Francisco area? I'll probably head down there around spring break with a couple of the Romanian kids.

Have you had any luck with photos yet? Did you get any from the guy in France? How about asking your uncle's friend to take some?

I got both of your letters. I hope things get better for you there. Keep writing and let me know how things go for you.

How is it in school? Did you make some new friends? Just be yourself and be good to everyone and things will get better.

Write soon, Sammy.

Love,

Bill

Box 16, 420 NW Ninth Ave., Portland, OR 97209

503-555-7678

It is time to move on, get on with it, hit the road. Sammy thinks this is not as much fun anymore. It was at some point, but now he finds it tedious. Sammy is still cute, but he needs something more interesting. He needs to widen his horizon. Sammy needs to move on.

Don't think for a minute that I don't know what you're thinking. Don't you think I know that it's bad? I'm not stupid, you know. So he is a pedophile. It is not my business. I'm not. Don't think that I am. I have never had sex with any boy at all, nor have I ever wanted to. The idea does not even remotely excite me. I am a homosexual. I like men, not boys. I even find it offensive that he considers himself gay. He gives gays a bad name, as if we needed that on top of all we have to deal with.

I'm not bad. I just enjoy being a precocious twelve-year-old. Why would I want to be a precocious forty-year-old?

Now the question that you should be asking yourselves is, Do I like the people I interact with? Do you think I do? How could I? They're sickos. Real sickos. Some of them can be nice, but they are still sickos. Bill is definitely a sicko. He is a perv. He is too. But I like talking to him. I liked, I no longer do. It's not my fault. If you were in my situation, you would too. He is a perv, but he can be an entertaining one. At least in the beginning he was. As the letters kept coming, he began to sound like a one-note samba: more photos, more photos.

You think I have no morals. You think I have no conscience. When the man told me he was writing to another fifteen-year-old boy in southern California, don't you think I felt awful? How I dealt with it was by assuming the other boy was also fictional. Maybe he was not, but then I can't do anything about it. Could I call the police and tell them this pedophile was trying to seduce a boy and I found out about it because I am jealous of this other boy? This is too sick. He now says Sammy is the only boy he is writing to so maybe the other boy was fictional too. It has to be that way. How could it be otherwise? He must have been fictional.

Oh, I'm tired.

Hi Sammy,

How are you? Why haven't you written since we spoke? It was a long time ago. What is the matter?

As I wrote to you often, I'd really like to not only write but also meet you in the near future.

Did you write to the boy whose address I sent?

How are you doing with your brother and father? Is your brother still acting like he was before?

How are things in school and on the soccer team? Do you like the school? What are your favorite classes? Soccer—are you having fun?

Please call me collect whenever you want and write as soon as you can, Sammy. I really want to stay friends with you.

Please remember to send me pictures of all of you.

Love,

Bill

Box 16, 420 NW Ninth Ave., Portland, OR 97209

503-555-7678

Sammy is charmingly forgetful. He gets easily distracted sometimes. Not from important things necessarily, but from writing letters for example. When he isn't as interested any longer, he gets somewhat forgetful. Hopefully he will outgrow this habit, but for now it is part of his charm. It makes him more human. If he did not have some failings here and there, he would be too perfect. He just forgot. It is not that big of a deal.

Sammy is an emotionally abused child. Not in the traditional sense. He does not have the classic symptoms. He is way above that. He is not scarred in any way. He functions very well in his environment. His parents abuse him, but he handles it, which only goes to show his amazing character. He really is a one-of-a-kind boy. Why do his parents abuse him? Because it makes Sammy more sympathetic, and a good man would want to save him and maybe even take care of him. It really is a very simple formula, which has been used over and over again.

Why do I keep doing it? I don't know. I would die of boredom otherwise. But then again, it's not like I am not dying of boredom. All in all, it's a pleasant way to spend a couple of hours.

So I spend a lot of time answering mail, talking on the phone, and logging on-line. So what? It is human contact and we all need that. Why do you think I would not need that? Don't I have the same needs as everyone else? I do. I have the same social needs. I need to reach out to people as much as you do. I can't spend all my time watching television. So I keep doing it. I am sure I would become completely nuts if I did not do it. It does not matter how much time it takes. I enjoy doing it.

Dear Bill,

I got your last letter. I am sorry I haven't written sooner. Things haven't been going great. Also school is keeping me very busy. But I'm sorry I haven't written before. I should have.

How are things with you? In your letter you asked if I was writing to the boy whose address you sent. You never sent me an address of any boy. Who is he? The only one I wanted to write to was Tomas, but then it turned out you wrote that card so that's okay. Is this the other boy you told me you were writing to?

I also wanted to call you. I tried a couple of times, but you were not in. I felt a little weird the last time we talked 'cause you sounded like you were a little busy and I didn't want to bug you.

My brother is still a major jerk. We're still not talking, and everybody still blames me. But I am not letting him touch me. My dad even hit me again because I would not make up with him. But that's okay 'cause I don't like them all.

School is going well. All the teachers think I am great. I still don't have many friends. But there is a boy who likes me. He's Thai and his name is Pol. He's fifteen and a sophomore. We play soccer together and we spend time together. He's really cute and I like him and he likes me.

My uncle is upset with me 'cause I went through his porno magazines again. He keeps hiding them but I always know where they are. I have been trying all kinds of stuff from the magazines. I tell my uncle about them and he freaks! He's so funny. I also think he is falling in love with another man, not his lover. It's kinda weird.

Tell me all about you. How are you living with all the Romanian boys? Are any of them cute? Do you like any one of them?

Again, I am sorry I have not written before but I have been really busy. You can write me as often as you like. I'm having some problems over here, but I should be able to deal with them (I want to poison the whole lot of them).

I think about you a lot. Do you think of me?

Bye now,

Sammy

Sammy is Lebanese. Why is that so? Because I am Lebanese. With Sammy, I sent my own picture as a twelve-year-old. I am Lebanese.

When pictures are not involved, the boys are European, Thai, whatever. They are never American. There are many reasons for that. Primarily, it is exotic. Just as important, for most pedophiles, fucking a foreigner seems to be more acceptable. You know, American kids are so immature. We foreign kids have a more accepting attitude towards sex. We foreign kids look forward to getting fucked by fat old men. Think about it.

I blame my failure in life on my acne. When I reached fifteen, my whole face broke out with severe acne. I was a beautiful boy. I turned ugly. Whatever potential I had disappeared with the first zit. You don't believe me, I know. I guess you never had acne. It completely takes over your life. It took over mine.

Very few people looked at me the same way after the acne came. More important, I never looked at me the same way. I know what you are thinking. You are thinking that a lot of people have been scarred by acne and they did not turn out to be perverts. That is such bullshit. We are all perverts. Most acne-scarred men hide it better. So do I. I decided to share this with you; without it you would have considered me a normal man. Okay, maybe not completely normal, but you would not have judged me as harshly as you are doing so now.

I still carry the scars. All of my face is pockmarked. I think it is the main reason I never had a relationship. Hell, I wouldn't want to wake up every day to a crater-face like mine. Why should someone else? I remember the girls giggling. I remember the boys shunning me. I remember the harsh words. Sticks and stones may break my bones, but words broke my soul. I was a happy-go-lucky boy and then I became a recluse.

Cystic acne. I used to get it all over my body. Now I only get a few. In those days, however, they were all over. My face was the most embarrassing. The worst part was that if I got one anywhere near my lips, they would swell to three times their size. When that happened, I was called nigger, even though I had blue eyes. If I got a cyst anywhere near my eye, it swelled shut. I would have to wear an eye patch to cover it up. I was called Moshe Dayan.

I started withdrawing from life. It was not my fault. Life wanted a certain look. I did not fit. Blame life, not me. I wonder sometimes what would have happened to me if my skin had not failed me. I would probably have been something. I would probably have been hired at all those job interviews. I could have been somebody.

Fuck you. I know what you're thinking.

Hi Sammy,

I'm glad you finally wrote. I was starting to worry about you. I thought that something had happened to you. Sounds like the same rotten stuff at home. Too bad. That's where you should feel the best and get a lot of love. I wish you were here where it would be a completely different situation. I think we would have a great time together.

I'm glad to hear that you like school and teachers like you. That helps in a new school. You mentioned about your Thai friend. Have you gotten together with him alone yet? Do you think he would like to do something with you sexually? Is he as cute as you? Hard to believe.

What kind of things in your uncle's magazines have you tried? What did you like best? What do you think would be the most fun to do when we get together?

There are three Romanian kids here now. One is cute, but they are all straight, I guess. All are good kids and I like them all. One works thirty-five hours per week at a fast food place. The other two help me with the construction work and do odd jobs here and there for friends.

In mid-December I plan to go to Texas to visit my mom for two to three weeks. After that I hope to get to Cuba and also perhaps Mexico, Honduras, and El Salvador. I'll come back about mid-March. At least those are the plans now.

I hope to get to California around springtime or early summer. You never wrote how I would be able to contact you fast when I travel to San Francisco. Is there a way to call you at home or something?

If you'd like to write to Tomas, I can send you the address. You can't tell him or anyone about us or about us being gay. Okay? You say that I'm a family friend and that you like to write to kids in other countries. Okay? Let me know the next time you write.

You are the only one I am writing to now, Sammy, so let's write more and feel free to say anything.

I'd like to get together with you when I get back from the winter trip.

How is your soccer team doing? How about you on the team? Do you start? What position? What is your Thai friend like physically? Can you describe him? Do you shower together after practice? Why don't you try to take a slow shower someday when he's in there. If you are the last two, maybe you could do something together in the shower. Do any of the kids ever jerk off or do anything together in the showers?

Write soon, Sammy. Let me know about Tomas and how you're doing.

Love,

Bill

Box 16, 420 NW Ninth Ave., Portland, OR 97209

503-555-7678

The best time to call me is probably Sunday evening—
if possible. On Monday and Wednesday night I play soccer.
Is it possible to call Sunday night (about 10:30?) or is it too
late?

Also please send a picture of all of you. Please.

Sammy is a wonderful boy. So is Pol. Pol is Thai. He likes Sammy.
Pol is fifteen, a couple of years older than Sammy, but physically
comparable. Sammy and Pol are having sex. Sammy thinks it is not
exactly what he wants, and he tells his friend in Portland as much.
He tells his friend he really prefers men. He enjoys being with Pol
and they do have a wonderful time together, but he always looks at
older men. His friend asks Sammy if Pol might want to get together
with both of them. Sammy learns of the term *ménage à trois* for the
first time. Sammy is learning so much.

So you think it is easy, do you? Do you think you could do it? I am
a natural-born actor. When I talk to the guys on the phone, I become the character. I believe what I am saying. I rarely get in trouble. I screw up when I say I am Hungarian and someone turns out
to speak the language. I have to think fast. That's what I am really
good at. Thinking on my feet—well, lying down to be exact. My feet
hurt a lot. I am really creative. Other problems occur when they ask
me what I am taking at school. How the fuck would I know? I never
went to high school over here. How would I know, for example, kids
are taught driver's ed at school? Sometimes I send pictures of young
models to men on America Online claiming they are me. I would
collect a whole series of pictures of the same guy. Some are fully
clothed, but most are naked. Every now and then someone would
realize that he had seen my picture before. I would be shocked and
demand he tell me where he had found it or who had sent it to him,
because someone had been circulating my picture. By the end of

the conversation, I get a full promise that he will never betray me by sending my pictures to anybody. He also agrees with me that most men are creeps and should not be trusted.

I am amazing at deception. I'm a natural.

Hi Bill,

I just got your letter. Thanks for writing. I'm sorry I had you worried. I didn't mean to worry you. But I'm glad you care about me. It's still the same kind of things at home. I hate it here. I can't wait to grow up and leave here. I wish I could leave now, but I can't figure out how to do it. I know if I were with you, it would be a completely different situation. I wish I could be with you. I really do. I think about it all the time. I think about living with you all the time. But I can't see how I can get up there. I'll call you this Sunday and we can talk.

Your trip sounds great. Wish I could go with you. I have my passport!

Let's see. You asked about Pol. He's fifteen. He's really cute. He's only an inch taller than I am. He's got black hair and brown eyes. He's got oriental eyes. Really cute. He's very skinny, although he eats a lot. He has no hair except a little on his dick, which is funny because he likes it that way. I don't. He says it is because he is Asian that he does not have a lot of hair. He doesn't even have hair under his arms yet. Still, he has more than I do because I don't even have hair on my dick yet. I told you I still look for it under a magnifying glass and can't find anything. Pol thinks that it's great that I don't have any because he doesn't like it at all. I'm the complete opposite. Pol's dick is also not very big. He's only a little bigger than mine.

Your suggestions about the showers were pretty good,

but it's okay 'cause we already have sex sort of. He started it. He asked me to come sleep at his house and we slept in the same bed and at night he started playing with my dick. He really only likes to suck me off. I do him but not as much as he does me. He doesn't like anything else 'cause when I told him I wanted to try fucking, he said it was gross. That's really silly, but that's what he likes and he says he likes to suck me off all the time, which is okay by me. Really that's all we do 'cause most of the time he doesn't even like me to play with his dick. I like that, but I want more I'm sure.

About my uncle's magazines. I haven't been able to try everything because I don't have anybody to try them with, but I have tried a number of things for jerking off. I saw a magazine with this guy who sucked his own dick and it looked really great so I have been trying to do it. I'm almost there. I can bend all the way backwards, with my feet way behind my head but I can only reach the tip of my dick with my tongue. If my dick gets a little bigger or I am able to be a little more flexible, then I will be able to suck my own dick, but right now I can lick the tip a bit and I can shoot in my mouth, which is really great. When I told my uncle I could do that, he freaked. He thinks he is turning me into a sex maniac, which is really funny. I also learned to squeeze my balls when I jerk off and also learned how to put my finger in my ass.

I have been going through all his magazines. He has some really cool ones. He keeps trying to hide them, but I know him so well that I know where he hides them. Even if he locks them up, what he doesn't know is that when he asked me to make a copy of his house key, I made a copy of all his keys so I can find the magazines wherever he hides them. He has a magazine, which has a guy shaving another guy. The guy getting shaved ends up completely without hair except on his head, which is just like me. It looked really cool to be shaved. There are a couple of magazines with a lot of leather, which I like. I like the men in those 'cause they have lots of muscles. In one magazine this really hot guy ties another guy up. The guy who is tied up is not so hot, but the guy who tied him up is so hot. Anyway, he tied him up and made him first suck his dick, which really turned me on. He then tore all his clothes off and spanked his ass really hard. He then whipped him, which I didn't think would be too great, but then in the end he fucked him and that looked like the best. He also has a lot of magazines about rimming, which is when you lick a guy's butt, which are really cool and I like them.

As to what would be the most fun to do when we get together, that's easy. I want to kiss you for a long time. Pol does not like to kiss and all he likes to do is suck me off. I want you to hold me for a long time and kiss me all over. I also want you to fuck me. That's what I like best. I want you to fuck me all the time in all kind of different ways. If you do that, then I will do whatever you want. I also want to suck you off all night and rim you too, but most of all I want you to fuck me. I wish you were here and I would do that all the time. What would you like to do?

About Tomas. I don't really want to write him now. I thought he was the one who wrote me, which is why I asked for his address to write him back, but since it was you who wrote that, I don't need to write to him.

Anyway, I had better go now. I really wish I could go and live with you. I would be really happy with you and would make you happy too. I'm really a nice boy. It's just that my brother is a jerk and my parents don't like me, that's all. But anyway, I had better go now. Please write soon. I promise I won't wait so long to write you again. I think of you all the time.

    Bye now,
    Sammy

Remembering is the disease I suffer from. It breaks my soul. It destroys my body.

Fools, I scream at the television. You fools. Some gorgeous boy comes on hawking his program for increasing memory. You can remember more, he tells us. You can remember everything. A curse falls on your house too, you son of a bitch. Why would I want to remember more?

My father calling my name loudly. My mother, the lush, following suit. Come out. Come out and meet our guests. All drunk. This is our boy. He came in second in his class. Second among one hundred and fifty students. Second, but not first. He will be first next term, won't you, boy? Show them how you play the recorder. Show them. He knows all the capitals of the world. Just name a country and he'll tell you its capital. Come on, what's the capital of Madagascar?

Everything comes back. It never really went away. Where would it go? It's all in my mind. It stays there forever.

I would be sitting down watching television and I would start remembering. Out of nowhere, my fucking mother comes back to me in full color. She persists in ruining my life. Dead and buried, after all these years, she comes into my life to tell me how I fuck everything up. Why does she torment me so?

I remember too much.

I sit on my father's lap. You'll always be my little boy. The stink of gin still haunts me. You are the best little boy in the world. You will make me proud. You will make your dad proud. The taste of fear, somewhat metallic, tickles my tongue. It takes a while to dissolve.

The persistence of memory is the bane of my existence, the blight of my life.

It never fails. The sound of snickering is my constant companion. I never forget.

Antananarivo.

In your dreams, ugly face. The twinkie said that to me. He was lying on the bed facedown, his ass an open invitation for anyone. For anyone else, not me. I walk into his room. He laughs and says, "In your dreams, ugly face." Fuck you. Fuck you. Why do I still remember all this? It was so long ago. He was shit-faced. Men kept going into his room. I would hear his moaning. Someone would come out and another would go in. Everyone, but not me. Piss on him. Piss on him. That fucking slut. Why do I keep remembering him?

Remembering is the disease I suffer from. After I remember, I get a fever. My mind clouds. A throbbing headache overcomes me. I feel numb in my extremities. Worst of all, I get severe diarrhea. I get overcome with memory at all times.

The persistence of memory is killing me.

Sammy is unhappy. Things are not working out the way he thinks they should. His parents are not understanding. He has no friends. He needs someone to guide him. He needs someone to help him. He needs someone to be there for him. He needs someone to be a complete friend. Sammy is asking for help.

Dear Sammy,

Just a note to tell you I am thinking of you. Wish you were here. I hope everything is working out better for you

now. I look forward to seeing more of you soon. I am planning to visit San Francisco as soon as I can.

Love,

Bill

I have always been someone else, always. Even as a child, I was
someone else. Every child has fantasy roles, but with me, they were
more than fantasy. They were as real as my real life. I was meticulous in my fantasies. I not only became the greatest basketball
player to have ever walked the face of the earth (being the greatest
player in the world now was not good enough), I had every detail of
my life as a basketball player figured out. Who my parents were,
what were the major events that had influenced my life, what I
would say when interviewed on television, etc. Every detail of my
fantasy life was well planned. Meticulous attention to detail was my
specialty. As I grew older and became more creative, my roles became much more complex. I was not only the greatest basketball
player to have ever walked the face of the earth, but also the best
musician, and the most perfectly beautiful human as well.

What seems interesting to me now is that my fantasy figures
were always under sixteen. Even as I grew older, the figures I was
fantasizing never grew older. I think that means something.

If I told you for example that, during the Olympics, I would always dream of myself as a gold-medal winner, you would say that is
normal. Everybody does. Well, I am not everybody. I am a much
more complex person. My dreams were not as simple as most
people's. No, I never fantasized about winning one gold medal, always nine or ten and all before my fifteenth birthday and after writing my first opera (which is not athletically related, but was an
important detail nonetheless). Even though I am not very patriotic,
I always fantasized myself as still being Lebanese, so the national
anthem had to be played during the medal ceremonies. I would
plan in detail how the Atlanta crew would search forever trying to

find a tape of the Lebanese anthem when I won my first gold. In Barcelona, they did not have to search because they were more organized. That is the kind of meticulous detail I planned for. But you wouldn't understand.

Hi Sammy,

Merry Christmas and Happy New Year. I hope your holidays are full of joy. I wish you were here so that I could kiss you and hug you. I would make love to you in front of the fireplace all night. I am sure you would like that as much as me. I can't wait to see you in spring. I love you.

Love and kisses,

Bill

Most of the men are high school teachers or coach some kind of boys' team. It never occurred to me before, but now it seems obvious. If you like boys, you hang out where they hang out.

I sometimes wonder about the nature of their perversion. Who is the most perverted?

I once had a man offer one of my boys quite a bit of cash for a blow job. When the boy asked him how much, the man replied twenty dollars per inch. Since the boy had eight inches—he would have had more, but I figured, at fifteen he needed room to grow—that would make $160. The man told the boy he would not even have to drop his pants, just let the man take it out and go to work.

Another man offered quite a bit of money to see videotapes of the boy getting plowed by his father. Of course, the father filmed quite a number of sessions with his boy, just for his own enjoyment. The boy felt certain that if he took one of the tapes, his father would not miss it for a while.

I never figured out a way of getting the money though. It's not that I needed it. It's not that I wanted the perverts to lose their

57

money either. I don't know why I would want it. Maybe it is another form of validation. If they sent me the money, then it meant they really liked me.

I talk to men in all walks of life. Some are filthy rich, others are as poor as church mice. The one thing they have in common is they all like me. It makes me feel good.

A lot of the times, I have a boyfriend. Well, not exactly a boyfriend since that would make me unavailable. I have a fuck buddy. Usually, it's a married man. He has been fucking me for about a year. He met me in a mall and invited me to his house. His wife is an executive who leaves town at least once a month. He's great to me. He fucks me so well when we get together. He buys me all kinds of gifts. He takes care of me. The problem is I see him only when his wife leaves town. I am looking for someone who could spend more time with me. The reaction to my married man is varied. Some men choose to disparage him. He is an awful person, someone who is using me. Those men could offer me more and would treat me much better. My married man is a liar who would do whatever it takes to get into my pants. A horrible person they want to save me from. Others tell me he is great. They want to offer me more in terms of a relationship, but they appreciate that he cares so much about me. The latter group, I tend to like more. But they all like me.

It's not always about sex, you know. They talk to me about everything. I tell them about my family. Sometimes my family is great. Sometimes they are just jerks. My mother died when I was a little kid or my mother is the best psychiatrist in the city. It depends on what personality I want to have. My favorite is when I have a full family—father, mother, and two older brothers. I am the baby of the family and everybody loves me. I am the center of the family's universe. That's my favorite. My father owns a multinational consulting company and my mother is a brain surgeon. Both of my brothers are getting their law degrees. My father and my mother are constantly discussing whether I should go to law or med school. My father had a long talk with me. He told me about safe sex. He said both my partner and I needed to wear condoms. I was ten when he told me that. I was shocked. How did he know I liked guys? He smiled and said it's okay if I did. Boy, he sure is cool. I love my family and they love me.

Dear Bill,

I haven't received a letter from you in so long. Why have you not written? Don't you like me anymore? I hope you are not like everybody else. No one likes me anymore. I thought you were my friend. Why haven't you written?

Please write me. I don't think I can go on if you are not my friend anymore. Why doesn't anybody like me? I'm a nice boy, I swear. I can't understand why nobody likes me. I try to be nice to everybody, but everybody is mean to me. I try hard to be a friend, but nobody cares. It's not fair. I want to have friends. I have feelings too. Everybody treats me like a pariah. Everybody thinks they can treat me like shit. It's not right. Everybody can go to hell.

I am a nice boy. I like everybody, but everybody hates me. Why? Can you answer that question for me? Why does everybody hate me? What have I done? I don't deserve this shit. I don't. Fuck them. Fuck everybody.

You know, I am really disappointed in you. I thought you would be different, but you turned out just like the rest of them, you little shit. I don't need you. I don't need anybody. I have done fine on my own, thank you very much. I don't need you.

I don't know why I even bothered with you. You started out so nice, but then you turned out just like everybody else. Fuck you. Fuck you. You're such an asshole. Fuck you. I don't want to ever speak to you again. I will return all your mail unopened from now on. I hope you die, you dickhead.

You know what? I never liked you. I just pretended to like you. I never really liked you. I knew you were a jerk from the first time we talked. You're stupid too. I could tell that just by talking to you on the phone. You're stupid and you know what, you're ugly too. I lied when I said you were handsome. I was just trying to make you feel good. Those are not muscles. You're fat. You're stupid, ugly, and fat. So there. Live with that, you fucker. Do you think I care that you don't like me? I don't care.

I will never speak to you again. I am doing fine on my own. I am not lonely. You're such a jerk. I hope you rot in hell. You will rot in hell, I know that. I just hope it is soon, you little shit.

Eat shit and die, you motherfucker.

Bye now,

Sammy

The disease courses through my body. I feel it moving. I will probably die soon. I am sure you're smiling, thinking good riddance. Well, fuck you. You know, you are so judgmental. You are probably sitting down, sipping some drink while you read this, feeling smug and oh, so superior. I suffer while you sit back and enjoy it. You probably had it easy. How do I know that? you ask. How do I know so much about you? Don't you think I can tell who would end up reading this? I know more about you than you do. Oh, oh, he's a perv, you say. But do you ever look at yourself? Do you ever think about what made me the way I am?

You did.

Every time I think about you reading the letters, my blood starts to boil. I am so upset because you now feel you are better than me. Don't try to deny it. I told you I know you. I know what you are thinking better than you do. I know. I know you're the perv. I know that for a fact.

I can't go on anymore with this.

Joshua is a really nice boy. He is a fourteen-year-old Jew from Baku. He has been in this country for three years.

The Changing Room

On June 17, 1976, my mother lost her mind completely. The American ambassador, Francis E. Meloy Jr., fifty-nine years old, was assassinated in Beirut. Washington advised all Americans to leave Lebanon. My mother wanted me to leave that day. Where? She did not care. She wanted me out. My dad tried to reason with her. I was the only child. He wanted me to stay with the family.

I had always thought of my mother as a fairly even-keeled woman. She never once raised her voice, never screamed at me. Whenever I did something she disapproved of, she would look menacingly at me, her offending offspring, raising her left eyebrow slightly. That was all it took to scare me into complete submission. It even worked on my father. I also never thought of her as very religious. I never saw her pray, unlike my father, who tried to pray the required five times daily, but rarely managed more than two.

My mother would cook when upset or nervous. On June 17, 1976, my mother spent the entire day in the kitchen cooking *ghammeh*, which in itself was unusual. *Ghammeh* is a dish with all the entrails of a recently slaughtered lamb, all stuffed with rice, peppers, and meats. It takes forever to clean and cook. Yet my mother was making it, and we had no guests coming over for dinner. The meal could feed between eight and fourteen people, yet there were only three of us for dinner. The strangest thing was that it was a winter dish. Everybody knew that.

She was in the kitchen cooking, and talking to the Prophet. My father and I did not dare go in, but we could hear snippets of her conversation. "O Muhammad, this world is too crazy. Make it stop." I looked in every now and then only to find her beating her chest, talking to the ceiling, and trying to stir the pot at the same time. Her usually immaculate hair was disheveled. She was barefoot. The front collar of her dress was torn, though still attached to the dress, moving slightly with each breath. My father paced outside the kitchen. Like me, he had no clue what to do. For the fifteen months since the fighting had begun, my mother was the only one who had kept insisting things would get better.

There have been many theories as to when the Lebanese Civil War started. Most believe it was the Phalange ambush of a Palestinian bus in April of 1975. Some think it is when the Lebanese president Suleyman Franjieh ordered the military to attack the PLO in 1973. The world community did not approve of that attack, so the Phalange party decided to arm themselves, since they could not rely on the military to get rid of the PLO. Still others believe the war started with the killing of the political leader of Sidon, Ma'rouf Sa'ad. Personally, I consider the war started on June 17, with the death of Meloy. The tear in my mother's dress was the zero hour.

A month later, I was on my way to England. I moved from a war zone directly into hell. I was fifteen. Nothing prepared me for the cruelty of the English. That year, my uncle was kidnapped by the Phalange, tortured, and returned to us a mere shell of himself. They had kept him tied up and blindfolded in a chair for four whole days, so by the time he was released, he was terrified of sunlight. The boys in my neighborhood were killing each other, thinking their once best friends were now a threat to their way of life. My countrymen became unrecognizable. Still, that did not prepare me for the English.

I was placed in Milfield, a boarding school or what the English called a public school. Milfield was in Street, Somerset, a little town near Bath, named such because it really did have just one street. Two things existed in Street, a Clarks shoe factory and the school. I thought that was somehow appropriate. The English raised children the way they made shoes, a bland, unimaginative product, comfortable enough to be stepped on.

The house I slept in was called Orchards. All the houses had names, as if by being named, they would suddenly acquire character. I would walk alone every morning, up the hill, trying to make sure I got to the school cafeteria on time. If one was late, one was not fed. I was always late. I could not wake up earlier than ten minutes before I was supposed to be at breakfast. My mother was no longer there to wake me.

All the other boys would be out of the house. Every morning, I found myself walking up the hill, alone in cold, misty, English weather, trying to make a reasonable facsimile of a knot in my tie.

But I refused to run. I would not hurry. I walked up to school. I hated their breakfasts anyway. The first day at breakfast, I stood in line, trying to figure what was in each tray. I had grown up with my mother cooking breakfast. How could I even consider kippers and baked beans?

Every morning, as I walked up the hill, a man came running down the hill. He probably worked at the shoe factory. He always wore the same pants and sports jacket, one of those typically cheap ones with fake leather on the elbows. The jacket was never completely on his body. He always adjusted it and tried to comb his hair back, his tie askew. One day, after about two weeks at school, I made a sign, which said, in big red letters, HELP ME, I CAN'T

STOP! I flashed it at him the next day as he was running by. He did not even look my way. Kept running by.

I wanted to like England. Like many Lebanese boys, I grew up thinking of myself as European. I thought of Lebanon as too small, not really big enough to leave a sustainable mark on. I grew up in a family of writers and I wanted to be one. I did not want to write poems relating how a doghouse in the mountains of Lebanon was better than a villa in Monte Carlo. I wanted to write something universal, unearth the human condition in eloquent words. I wanted to write my name on the refulgent sky, tell the heedless world I had arrived. I thought of England as the land of Shakespeare, Hardy, and Dickens. I wanted to fit in.

I couldn't imagine listening to Arabic music, so I grew up with English bands. I thought David Bowie was the king of kings and I loved Queen. However, the band to whom I had dedicated my young life was Genesis. I had all their albums. I had built all my fantasies of England through them and their music. In my England, there were knights and damsels in distress, voluptuous queens and four-foot-tall men, watchers of the skies and magic kings.

Peter Gabriel would stand in front of the stage, looking lost and forlorn. His face all made up, a small portion of his hair shaved off at the front, he would sing, moan, and wail, recalling days of glory and magic. I wanted to be him. I wanted him to like me. He would stand in front of a bass drum, his foot pressing my lonely heart with each thump. My father once came into my room to complain about the loud music. He stood aghast when he saw me standing in front of the mirror, all decked out in black, with lipstick and eyeliner, holding a brush as a microphone, singing along to "Supper's Ready." He left shaking his head, another example of how young men were nothing like when he was growing up.

I was the only one of my friends who liked Genesis. I felt special. I would run every week to the newsstand and get a copy of *Melody Maker,* reading it religiously, trying to find any news of my idols. I used to wish I were in England where I would not have to wait for two days before the issue arrived at the stores. I wanted to be in the center.

Peter Gabriel left Genesis in the summer of 1975 when I almost had a nervous breakdown. That was a year before I arrived in England when I had to endure the Sex Pistols and Genesis with a sappy Phil Collins singing puerile songs. It was not the same, not the same at all.

Mrs. Troy, no first name, fortyish, frumpish, blond gray hair in a tight bun, met me at the airport. She looked questioningly at me as I came through customs. She held a card with my name on it, which made me feel important for a minute, at least until she smiled. It was so inexplicably fake.

"Is that you?" she asked, pointing at the name on the sign. I nodded. "I'm Mrs. Troy." That was all she said. She began walking away and I figured I had to follow. She drove me in silence to Maidenhead where my *adviser,* Mr. Boldwood, lived.

Everything was wrong. They dressed wrong, they smiled wrong, and they drove on the wrong side of the road. I completely forgot the steering wheel was on the right side, and when we arrived at the car, I had automatically walked to the wrong side. Mrs. Troy shook her head in consternation. I began to panic as we drove. London was too big and frightening. The crowds were strange, never smiling, and wore dull colors. Worst of all, the louring sky was menacing even though it was not yet winter. I realized writing my name across it would have to wait. I was scared.

Mr. Boldwood's house was Maynard's Cottage. He had arranged a profitable business for himself. He called himself an adviser and had over one hundred Middle-Eastern boys in his charge. His job was to place all these boys in boarding schools, making sure they did not get into a lot of trouble. His hobby, on the other hand, was trying to get any of the boys naked in his house. It seemed he was pretty successful. He showed me pictures when I arrived, in a failed attempt to entice me to undress.

At a very early age I knew I was different sexually. I knew I liked men, but I also knew I did not like Mr. Boldwood. He was old, doddering, malodorous, and like most Englishmen, I was about to find out, had absolutely terrible teeth. As nervous as I was about his persistent attention, I would have broken down and undressed for him if he had not reeked. I could not stand being in the same room with him. That was the extent of my courage. I was terrified of him, but I could not betray my olfactories. I had to live in his house until I left for Milfield.

On the last day at Maynard's Cottage, I smelled Boldwood before he came into the room where I was staying. He had figured I could not stomach his stench, probably because my nose kept wrinkling in his presence, so he had splashed some perfume on himself. He must have used the whole bottle because I could not breathe. By the time he sat next to me on my bed, I was visibly shaking. I had to hold my breath. The rank stench was unbearable. He put his hand on my quivering knee and said in an aged voice, "Do I frighten you?" Still holding my breath, I nodded. He moved his hand up my leg, and I could not hold my breath any longer. I violently exhaled, emitting a rather embarrassing sound. That was followed by a coughing fit that seemed endless. I ran and opened the window, putting my head out and breathing some fresh air. By the time the cough subsided and I turned around, Boldwood had left the room. I left for school that afternoon.

This story is not about Mr. Boldwood. He plays only a small part in it really. I wanted to bring him in briefly because it elucidates my situation. He was really my introduction to that vile country. I am not suggesting all Englishmen are pedophiles, although I am sure most of them are. I am suggesting that all of them are cruel, smug, and self-centered.

A total of eight other Lebanese boys were in the school, and they ended up hanging out together. All of them had come to the school the year before, when the fighting started. One rarely encountered a Lebanese boy alone. They were always in a group. I think it was the only way they thought they could survive the school. That created something of a paradox, because even though the mix was not always an easy one, the boys mingled irrespective of religion. The five Christian boys actually tolerated the non-Christians, and vice versa, which was obviously not the case in their homeland. One would not say they created interfaith intimate friendships, just an indulgent commixture.

They even included some other Arabs in the group, which was unnaturally tolerant. However, since the English shunned them all, they stuck together.

I was never really a part of that group. I had a couple of things going against me. First, I spoke English fluently, without a noticeable accent, and second, I had the bad sense of wanting to study English literature. When I first came to the school, I was ignorant of the accepted protocols of the various groups. Coming into the house after the second day of school, I had heard the music of Genesis coming out of the second-floor window. I was ecstatic. I ran up to the room. The door was open, but I knocked on the door anyway. Four English boys were lying on the two made beds, listening to the music. One of the boys looked at me and asked disdainfully, "What do you want?" I was taken aback, but still, I smiled and said, "I like

Genesis." I knew I should have come up with something more witty or deep. An indolent mouth screamed, "Piss off, you bloody wog."

That mistake would have been bearable if another Lebanese had not witnessed my humiliation. By the following day, the group considered my faux pas an unmitigated disaster. I figured the Lebanese boys would never really accept me because I was different, but this case proved much more than that. I was now a traitor.

I was alone most of the time. When I became too lonely, I hung around other outcasts, a couple of Americans, a Spaniard, or a Pakistani boy from South Africa called Munir. I also discovered glue. My roommate, an American junkie in a coat and tie, taught me the trick. Drugs were not readily available in the dull town of Street. We had to wait till some kid went for a weekend in London to score, which was often, but not often enough to alleviate sudden spells of utter boredom. Swiping a can of glue from the wood shop, however, was a piece of cake. I would sit in my room, take a huge hit of fumes, and black out. One night, I went into the sitting room with my can of glue and turned the television on. They were talking about the American presidential elections. Jimmy Carter's teeth were the last thing I remembered before blacking out. I dreamed of America. I dreamed of a place with blue skies to write my name across.

I noticed him about three weeks after Christmas break. Something about him caught my attention. He was normal looking for a Persian, could not have been more than thirteen. I was not sure what it was, but I knew he was different. I knew he liked boys, just like me.

His name was Cyrus.

The English called us all wogs. Since they were not creative enough to come up with a good insulting name for Middle Easterners, they lumped us with the Indians and Pakistanis. Wogs. The first time someone spat out that name at me, I was completely shaken. I sat in my room with pen and paper trying to figure out what it meant. Was it an acronym? The only thing I could think of was Western Oriental Gentleman. I knew that was not it. Someone explained it as being some shortened form of willywog or golliwog, but I doubt that was it. Looking through the unabridged Oxford English Dictionary, I found out no one knew where the term first originated. It was first used in print in 1929, to mean an Arab, someone with dark skin. Despite my being very light skinned, I was a wog, for now and forever.

I decided to ignore the name-calling. Whenever someone called me a name, I pretended not to hear. I handled it better than other Arab students. They became incensed. They would huddle together and plot revenge on an entire nation. They wished for a bigger oil embargo. They thought nuclear war, blow up the whole damn place. Still, as upset as they thought they were, it was nothing compared to the Africans. The English thought of them as the lowest life-form of all. They had numerous names for them—niggers, nig-nogs, spooks, chimney sweepers, you name it.

Once in the cafeteria, a table of English boys behind me, boisterous, were trying to outdo each other with names for black boys. Each boy would shout a more insulting one. It took a while before I noticed the boy from Cameroon sitting all alone at a table, like me. The boys were shouting to make sure he heard. He tried hard to make sure no one noticed he was crying.

I desperately wanted to go back to Beirut for Christmas. The war had ended in mid-November. Thirty-five thousand people had died. I talked to my dad and he said I would stay in England. The situation could erupt any minute, he told me.

I spent Christmas with a family in Maidenhead. That was much better than staying with Boldwood, for obvious reasons, not the least of which was they left me alone. I ended up baby-sitting their two little girls. The girls and I must have seen Disney's *Jungle Book* about eight times at the Maidenhead movie theater.

One day I took the train to London. At Victoria Station I saw Yehya, a boy I knew from school back home. Yehya was his last name. I never learned what his first name was. He was from Yemen. We were in the same class even though he was at least a couple of years older than I was. We never talked much when we were in Beirut. We hung around completely different groups.

I grew up idolizing Yehya. He was the best football player I had ever seen. He was a poet on the football field. He was short, about as tall as I was, except he weighed at least twenty pounds more than I did, all muscle. Everybody said if he were taller, he would have been a more impressive player, a natural forward. I thought they were full of shit. He was the best central midfielder in school. Every play had to go though him. Forwards may get all the glory, but he was the one who set everybody up. We played on opposing teams and I had to mark him. He was the most difficult player I ever played against. I adored him. I never thought he knew I existed. We were definitely not peers. At Victoria Station, however, we met as if we were best friends. I almost cried I was so happy. Ecstatic, because he was just as pleased to see me.

He asked me to visit him in Kent where he went to school. I could come play soccer with him. I told him I would love to since I had nothing to do for the entire holidays.

That Saturday, I went to see him. We played on the same team for the first time. It was incredible. It seemed we knew where the other was every single second of the game. We thoroughly trashed the other team. I did not recall ever playing in a better game.

At the end of the game, I was sitting on the grass changing my shoes. An English boy from the team I played on started talking to me.

"Isn't he a great player?" he asked me, nodding in Yehya's direction.

"He's the best," I said proudly.

"Yeah, all black boys are great athletes."

I was taken aback. I looked at Yehya over by the ice cooler and my face colored. I noticed for the first time he was black.

Starting at noon, when we broke for lunch, an Englishwoman would have her door open and you could see into her house. Whenever any of the boys walked down to Orchards after lunch, they would see the middle-aged woman in her negligee with her breasts hanging obscenely. She would smile at the boys, pretending to be doing something indoors, but in fact all she wanted was to be seen. She was deranged, that at least was obvious. By the second week, some boys got enough courage to approach her. They were amply rewarded for their initiative. Soon everybody figured out she liked to fuck young boys.

One day, I was walking down to the house with Munir, the Pakistani boy. As we passed by the house, the woman was in her doorway, one breast showing completely. Munir stopped in his tracks to stare. She looked at him and screamed, "What are you looking at, you bloody wog?" The more he blushed, the more she sneered.

I did not know what came over me. All of a sudden, I became furious. "He's looking at how ugly you are, you fucking slag," I screamed at her. Shocked, she mumbled something incoherent to herself and slammed the door shut.

Overnight, I gained some respect from the wogs.

The school had a disciplinary system utilizing students as prefects. Older students, if they were not troublemakers, were promoted to house prefects. They were responsible to the housemasters, who were teachers. The prefects could order us mere peons around.

Rules did not always apply to them. For example, they were allowed to smoke in their rooms.

I was in a strange situation. I was younger than most of the prefects, yet most of them were in my class, the lower sixth. Every student had a prefect who made his life miserable. Mine was Corey Whitehead. For two weeks, he went after me. He wanted me to shine his shoes. I argued that shining shoes was the job of younger kids. He would punish me by forcing me to stay in *the room,* which was nothing more than a room with terrible lighting. I could not read, listen to music, or watch television while I was in *the room.* I did not mind that punishment at all, which infuriated Whitehead. I had to find a way to deal with him or he would have devised a more severe punishment.

My English teacher was an old spinster named Miss Collins. She looked like the quintessential librarian, with pulled-back gray hair and glasses. I liked her, though, because we had one thing in common, a love for literature. Because I loved reading, I had already finished all the books for the class. When Miss Collins asked us to write an essay on something we loved, I wrote mine on Thomas Hardy's *Far from the Madding Crowd,* a book the class had yet to read. I did not have to exaggerate. I loved the book. I could not understand how such a sinister people could write so beautifully. My essay was really simple. I used the men's love of Bathsheba as a metaphor for my love of the book. It worked magnificently. Miss Collins showed up in class in a bright dress for the first time. She praised my essay. She lauded the fact that a nonnative speaker could write so beautifully. She mentioned her earlier reservations about a foreigner sitting for an English Literature A-level exam. Not in her wildest dreams could she imagine such style, such structure, from the pen of a non-Englishman. She had no doubts now. I was destined for great things.

I was grateful for her approbation to be sure, I told her, but the essay was not as well written as it could be, for you see, I had this prefect who was punishing me for no reason, for the simple fact that I was not English. I did not have enough time for my favorite pastime, writing and reading. Tears stained both our faces.

Poor Whitehead had no idea what hit him. Within a period of twenty-four hours, Miss Collins, both housemasters, and the schoolmaster screamed at him. I became someone not to mess around with, a sure seat for my S levels and a place in Cambridge. It wasn't just Whitehead who had to stay away, it was all the damn prefects. All the students had to give me breathing room. I was to be left alone. For a while, I became the fair-haired boy.

Cyrus's smile was his most memorable feature. It was more like a twitch. He seemed to be so desperately needy, he would nervously attempt a smile whenever anyone crossed his way. The corners of his mouth would try to meet his ears for a brief second before re-turning to their normal position, an ineluctable journey, for he was desperate and the other boys ignored him. Most of the boys, that is, not the prefects.

He was so obsequious, prefects roamed his skies like vultures. They had him running errands day and night. He was their maid-servant, their handmaiden.

I both pitied and hated him. I pitied him because he did not have many options. He was exactly the kind of boy the prefects liked to abuse—young, foreign, and not too bright. I hated him because he seemed oblivious to his shame.

I talked to him once. There was a fish-and-chips restaurant in the town. An Italian woman from Bari ran it. I asked her once if she served anything else since I did not like fish. She said she could make a spaghetti dish for me for fifty pence. It was better than anything served in the school cafeteria. Within a couple of weeks, she had queues of students waiting to eat at her place. One night, Cyrus was sitting at a table all by himself. The place was so crowded that everyone shared tables, except for Cyrus's table. I sat with him, which seemed to shock him. Introducing myself was all it took to hear his life story.

He was from a wealthy family from Tehran. He was the fifth son of eight. His father ensured that his sons got the best of everything. Cyrus only saw his father twice a year for he traveled all over. A well-loved nanny had raised Cyrus. He did not consider that strange. I asked him if any of his siblings were at the school. He said his father thought it would be better if Cyrus was immersed in English culture, and the presence of a brother would only make it more difficult. Each of his brothers was in a different boarding school.

I was eating my dinner, but he just went on talking, barely eating from the plate in front of him. He tried to convince me how much he liked the school. He was going to become an engineer, build grand bridges across seas. He was going to make his father proud. Milfield was a great step in the right direction. He was learning more than just schoolwork. He was acquiring discipline, and a successful attitude. All the boys he now knew were going to be important someday and would be invaluable contacts for him when he was an engineer.

He went on and on. In the middle of his dinner, two prefects came over and ordered him back to the house to iron their shirts. He left running. I never talked to him again.

I tried to play football at Milfield, but I did not last long. The English substituted aggression for skill, finesse, or intelligence. Every time I dribbled past an opposing player, he would take me down from behind. After every game, I would come back with black-and-blue bruises everywhere. That was not the reason I quit. Neither was the fact that none of my teammates ever came to my defense when I was hacked. I quit because of the bus ride. I got on the school bus and a Nigerian boy followed soon after. My teammates began to sing "I'm dreaming of a white Milfield" to the tune of "I'm dreaming of a white Christmas."

Rumors about my being queer began to surface about a week after I screamed at the town whore. The two incidents were not independent. Some English boys must have figured if I would scream at a woman, calling her names, I was queer. I was terrified, but did not answer the rumors. I would hear someone calling me queer as I passed by. I tried to ignore it. What's the difference between being called queer or wog?

Apparently, it was a big difference to my other outcast friends. They started avoiding me. It was strange. One day we were hanging out together and the next they were nowhere to be found.

The school stopped talking about me when it was found out that Cyrus was queer. With me, it was only hearsay. With Cyrus, it was found out he was giving blow jobs to a prefect. It was not really found out. One day the prefect, an upper-class twit called Brattleby, told everybody that Cyrus had been sucking his dick every night before he went to sleep. Cyrus was considered a bloody queer and Brattleby was a sly guy who had figured out how to get a blow job. Brattleby's housemaster did not even talk to him, but did, however, send a letter to Cyrus's father asking him to come down for a talk. That Brattleby was eighteen and Cyrus thirteen was never considered. Just as it was never considered that Brattleby, as a prefect, could order Cyrus to fellate him and the boy could not refuse.

It was decided that Cyrus was queer.

I was smoking in my room by then. If the prefects could do it, so could I.

———

I lost my virginity during Christmas break. So by the time the boys started calling me queer, I truly was. I had taken the train from Maidenhead to London. Boldwood had given me some pocket money to buy gifts. At Leicester Square, I used the public WC to pee. An Englishman was standing at the urinal with an erection. It mesmerized me. He winked at me and went to a stall. I followed. We started kissing and I dropped my pants. "No, no," he said, "I like doing that." He proceeded to lift my pants back up and drop them slowly. He buggered me right there. He waited till I ejaculated before running out of the stall. It was then I discovered not only had I lost my virginity, I had lost all my cash as well. Luckily, he left my return rail ticket.

Cyrus hanged himself in the changing room. News flew across the whole school. One of the teachers had walked into the room and found him swinging from the ceiling. The body was removed quickly and they barred entry into the room. Still, all the boys huddled outside the green door, which had THE CHANGING ROOM painted on it in big white letters.

Within an hour, someone had scratched out the C. The schoolmaster had a handyman come and paint the entire door before the day was out.

Cyrus killed himself two days before Easter break. The symbolism was lost on everyone, but me. I walked around in a trance. On the last day of the term, only two days after Cyrus was no more, Winthrop sat on the grass with Brattleby and two other prefects. I was walking to class when Winthrop said, "Hey there, pooftah." What I usually ignored, I couldn't anymore. He was smiling, smirking really, thinking he was a clever little shit. I kicked his head so hard he went unconscious. Years of football had come in handy. He flopped sideways. But I did not stop there. I jumped on Brattleby and began pummeling him. I did not care where I hit. I just did.

The other two boys did not let me do what I really wanted to do. I wanted to break every bone in his face. I was too small and much younger than both of them. They picked me up and away from Brattleby. Before they got a chance to beat me to a pulp, two teachers showed up to control the situation.

Nonetheless, when Brattleby stood up and I saw his face, I screamed. I felt so proud. He had a split lip, a broken tooth, and blood was all over his face. I could not help myself. I taunted him. I did not know what I was saying. I jumped up and down, pointing my finger at him, then at everybody who was there. I told him to go tell his mom a faggot had beaten him up. I told him to go hide because a queer wog was better than him at everything. I made sure to threaten everybody with the same fate if anybody dared call me any name after that day. I was the champ. I was the king. For a few minutes, I was the fair-haired boy.

I was suspended for a week. They thought that was punishment. They wanted to kick me out, but Miss Collins threatened retirement. I spent that week and Easter break in Paris at a friend's house. They were richer than we were and the whole family had moved to Paris. I decided I liked the French more than the English. They may be assholes and rude, but at least they knew they were.

Back at school, things were never the same. A new rule was instituted. If anyone called another person a derogatory name, he was suspended. I did not have to worry whether a rule was in place or not. All the English boys avoided me. There used to be this thing where if a boy wore a pink shirt, all the other boys told him it meant he was queer. I bought three pink shirts to make sure I never ran out.

I was supposed to give a short speech at the end-of-term dinner. Miss Collins had volunteered me to represent the foreigners at the school. I had the speech written the week before, but I did not think I could do it without mentioning the hanging room, without telling them all to go fuck themselves. As it turned out, I didn't have to worry about it. One teacher came up to me and said that a queer boy would give an end-of-term speech over his dead body. I asked him if he had not been dead since the fifties anyway.

A Kuwaiti was given the *honor* of giving the speech. The speech was dull, as dull as mine would have been. At the end, I heard him say, "And I would like to end my speech by blessing you all in Arabic." In Arabic, the Lebanese dialect, not Kuwaiti, the boy looked at me and said, "Eat shit and die a miserable death, all you English sons of dogs." He said it all with a smile on his lips. I could see all the Arab students stand up and cheer. I was on my feet. We were looking at each other, ecstatic. All the other students and teachers followed suit, applauding the sentiment.

I never made it back the following year. I never made it to Cambridge either. I went to UCLA of all places, to Los Angeles, where being different was part of the landscape. I found my bright sky. I never went back to the school or cared to know what happened to any of the people there. I avoided England for a long time, trying to put it all behind me. It took a long time to be able to write *color* without the *u*.

Duck

"You're deth-th-th-picable!"

Energetic More like frantic. The duck is frantic. A black mass bouncing off the walls. Daffy is the ultimate New Yorker. His eyes, the most prominent features. Constantly searching. Constantly accusing.

Walking home. Cold. Seventh Avenue is too crowded. What am I going to do? There is hope. There is hope. They tell us there is hope.

The duck did not know what happened. It did not plummet. I thought it would plummet. A quick dive. A plunge. No. It fluttered. Wings flapped, not knowing what happened. Tried to keep flying. It fluttered. Kept dropping.

The nurse changes the sheets. Jim had another accident. Luckily, she is here to help. The third accident in twenty-four hours. Where it is coming from is beyond me. He has not been able to drink anything for two days.

I sit in the dark, pondering my fate. I can still hear Jim breathing. How long?

"It has started."

"What do you mean?" She knows what I mean. I am not sure whether she wants me to be more specific to overcome my denial or hers.

"The results of my blood tests are back," I say with profound equanimity.

"Oh, my God. Oh my God," she keeps repeating.

"I miss you. I wish you would come visit us soon."

"I can't do it now, Mother. Hopefully soon. Are you all doing all right?"

"Yes, we're doing fine."

"Did you get my check?"

"Oh, yes we did. That was much more than we needed."

"That's okay. Enjoy it."

"Are you sure you can afford it?"

"I'm sure, Mother. If you need anything, you just have to ask."

"But you send us enough already."

"I'm not sending as much money as you think, Mother; it just goes further over there. I told you, I make a lot more than I need."

"That's because you don't have a family."

"I know, I know. We've been through this before, Mother."

"Well, it's just that there is this girl."

New York. Hama. Hama was the first big city I ever visited. My dad took me along. So many people. They could fit all the people of my village in one building. It took five more years, till I was ten, for my first visit to Damascus. Now I live in New York.

I remember your touch, your kiss, your warm embrace. Your song plays in my head all day.

———

Daffy in Ali Baba's cave. "It's mine," he screams. "It's mine. All mine, mine, mine, mine." He dives into the treasure. "I'm ritthh. I'm ritthh. It's all mine, mine, mine."

Jim laughs hysterically. He's seen this so many times. He still laughs.

Cold. The wind picks up. If Jim dies soon, I might be able to fly somewhere warm to relax.

Cold. It's so cold this early in the morning. I am not supposed to be making any noise. I sit still. Cold. Wet. The Euphrates rolls along, making noise, but I can't. Dad is crouching, hidden behind the reeds, gun ready. Gurgle, gurgle. The river keeps moving.

Cold, but the people adjust. They keep moving. Life keeps moving. Hordes of people pass me by. Do they care that my viral load is ninety thousand?

Cold. Jim shivers. I have a feeling this is the last time he'll walk outside. Slowpoke Gonzalez. Weight on the cane. Blue-toned skin. The leather chaps look ridiculous on his skinny legs.

I no longer sleep in our bed. A month ago I graduated to my own room. For the first time in thirteen years, I slept in a different bed than Jim. I let him keep all the stuffed animals.

Invirase. Better known as saquinavir. Two-hundred-milligram capsules. Take three capsules by mouth three times daily. The manufacturer recommends this medication be taken within two hours after a full meal. This medication is used to manage the infection of the human immunodeficiency virus (HIV), and other conditions as determined by your doctor. This medication will not prevent you from spreading HIV through blood or sexual contact.

My dad said I am to accompany him on this hunting trip. Make a man out of me, he said. My mother said I was too young. He said I was too effeminate and needed to toughen up.

"But your immune system is still holding up?" she asks imploringly.

"Yes, it is. For the time being. I have a high viral load, though."

"But that's not too bad. With the new protease inhibitors, they have been able to get great results. You should be fine."

"Laura, dear. I have to take these fucking pills for the rest of my fucking life."

"I know, but you can think of yourself as a diabetic or something."

"Laura," I scream, "if I were a diabetic, I would not have a problem getting into Syria."

A martini. I made myself a dry vodka martini and sat in the dark.

Thwapp. He slaps me hard.

"You're deth-th-th-picable!"

Daffy is hyper as usual. He jumps around the house. His eyes challenging me. "You're deth-th-th-picable!" He looks around my apartment. His eyes light up. "It's mine," he says. "It's all mine, mine, mine, mine, mine." He begins to collect our possessions in his arms. "Mine." He takes everything. Soon the apartment is almost empty. Then he walks into Jim's room.

———

This is not the man I love. Whatever happened to the man I love?

Epivir (3TC) 150mg tablets. Take one tablet by mouth twice daily. Be sure to tell your doctor if the following occur:

Persistent fever or sore throat, shortness of breath, unusual weakness, dizziness, abdominal pain, nausea and vomiting, pain, or numbness in hands or feet, skin rash, yellowing of the skin, abnormally dark urine, or any other unusual, bothersome effect.

I open the door. Something is wrong. It takes a few seconds to figure out what. Neither of the cats comes to greet me. They could be lying somewhere, avoiding the heat. I call. I hear a ruckus. A bird comes flying by. Both cats are jumping, following it. It flies straight into the only closed window in the apartment. Trumpet jumps on it when it falls. Holds it in his teeth. Turnip tries to see what it looks like. I run and get Trumpet to release it. I hold the bird in my hand. It appears unhurt. I can feel its heartbeat. Tiny little thing. Only the little head shows from my hand.

I place the bird on my fire escape. It does not fly away. It does not know what has happened. I watch. Five minutes later. I decide to check out whether it can fly. When it sees me move, it flies.

Cold. The river rolls along. I sit shivering noiselessly. My dad waits. He lights a cigarette. I watch the amber glow. The sun is not out yet. It's cold. We're waiting for the ducks. I look at the gun.

I look at the gun. Jim's handgun. I have never fired one before. Maybe it's time. I hold it. I point it at my temple. It might slip. In my mouth.

———

Cold. I sit in the dark. In a cold, analytical fashion, I try to figure out what happened to my life.

"But there is hope, dear. It's not a death sentence anymore. You must have hope."

The sun is still not out, but I can see better. I can see my older brother crouching behind the reeds. I figure if I can see him, the ducks can. He's eleven now and has a gun for the first time. He lights a cigarette when my dad does. I guess he thinks my dad can't see him.

I wake up because I feel something is wrong. The chair hurts my back, but that's not it. Christ! Jim has stopped breathing. How long has it been? I come closer. He violently exhales.

Bang. Woohoo. Bang. Woohoo. Bang.

I shoot Daffy in the butt. He runs around the room. No matter where I point the gun, I always hit his butt. He keeps holding it and revealing it at the same time.

I look at the gun. Dispassionately. In a cold, analytical fashion.

I told my doctor I refuse to take AZT. I saw what it did to Jim. I believe AZT killed him, not AIDS. He gave me DDI instead. I lost that argument.

Cold. I shudder perceptibly. My dad frowns. Toughen up, he scowls. He lights another cigarette. His mustache gleams.

Cold. I shudder perceptibly. Jim smiles at me. "I can warm you up, you know!" Best come-on line I've heard. On Seventh Avenue no less. Hordes of people pass us by, uncaring. People keep moving. I smile back, unsure what to say. He takes my arm and leads me to his place. I fell in love with him that first time.

On an empty stomach. At six in the morning. I swallow one 3TC pill. I then chew two 100mg tablets of DDI. It tastes like shit. It upsets my stomach. I go back to sleep.

Jim asks for an apple, sliced. He refuses to have a strained one. I hate him.

"Is there anything else, Mom?"

"Well, yes. Your brother is too proud to ask. His shop is not doing very well right now."

"His shop has never done well, Mom. How much this time?"

Daffy takes Jim's IV stand. "It's mine, mine, mine."

The ducks come. My brother stands. Aims his gun. Shoots. Misses completely. Scares the ducks. They veer towards my dad. He stands. Aims, shoots in one motion. I saw a duck get hit. It did not plummet.

Cold. The barrel in my mouth is cold.

I wanted to be someone. I was much too smart for my backwater school. I worked for Wang computers when I graduated. They moved me stateside, committed suicide, and left me to fend for myself in New York.

Jim slowly wastes away before my eyes. Into death.

———

"Toughen up," Jim says.

"I'm not sure I can." I weep uncontrollably.

"I need you to be strong," he says weakly. "For me."

I would try the medications for a week. Five times a day I have to train my throat to swallow pills. The week is up. My throat refused.

How will I go on without you?

How will I sleep without you?

Who will love me?

Who will care for me?

Bang. The gun explodes. A duck falters. It struggles. It doesn't plummet. It tries to fly. Flaps its wings. Desperately flaps its wings. Desperate. It falls gradually.

Thwapp. He slaps my face. It hurts like hell. Tears well up. Turn the other cheek. Slowly. He likes it slow. Thwapp. Jim slaps my face again.

"Crybaby, crybaby." My brother jumps on the bed. Taunting. I can't even cry in peace. This is his bed. He always makes that clear. I only sleep on it. He jumps on the bed. I feel my prone body leave the bed in rhythm. "You're such a girl." Up. Down. Up. Down. Up.

The Syrian secret-service agent pushes the customs officer aside. He looks at me disdainfully. He opens my bag. I run things over here, he says. What are all these pills? Do you have AIDS? You dare bring AIDS into our country? You're despicable. Whooo . . . hooo . . . hooo . . . hooo . . . hoooo . . . hooooohooo . . . hoohooo. The agent does somersaults.

At eighteen, my brother married the daughter of the most important man in the village. She was younger than I, fourteen. The marriage, which was supposed to improve our family's fortunes, did not, even though my brother got a store as a wedding gift from his in-laws.

Jim slaps my ass. Harder. "To whom does this ass belong?" Correct grammar. English professor, after all. "It's yours, sir," I whimper. "It's mine, mine, mine, mine, mine, mine." Thwapp.

Thwapp. He slaps my face. It hurts like hell. Tears well up. I try to control them. My father looks at me sternly. I'm about to cry. "You're despicable."

"Ouch. You fucker."
    "I'm sorry," I say.
    "Can't you find the fucking vein?" Jim is boiling mad. He hasn't been able to move for two days now.

The gun tastes strangely. Not as metallic as I thought. I dunk it into the martini and put it back in my mouth. Much better.

Your body, once so responsive, refuses to be aroused, refuses to be warmed, refuses to be revived.

The duck hits the ground. Tries to fly up once more. Daffy does somersaults. "It's mine, mine, mine, mine, mine."

The duck hits the ground. Tries to fly up once more.
    "Go get it," my father tells me.
    "Me?"
    "Yes, you," he screams. "Get your ass over there and bring it here."

Jim fell. I was sitting in my chair reading when I heard the sound. A thud, Jim falling, followed by a crash, his IV stand. He was on the floor in front of the bathroom door. His walker was still erect. He tried to get up before I got there, but to no avail. "I just wanted to use the bathroom," he complained. The IV bag broke. Jim was soaked. He had a deep bruise right above the knee where he fell. He looked so helpless.

The duck is in the mud. The river rolls along next to it, uncaring. The duck is still alive. It sees me and tries to flee. It cannot really move anymore. Helpless. Lonely. I stare at it. I start crying. "Get the fucking duck," my dad screams. It is the duck or me. I try to pick up the duck, but it moves. I end up falling in the mud. I finally catch it. I hold the duck in my hands. I can feel its heartbeat.

"I miss you. I wish you would come visit us soon."

"I wish I could, Mother. I can't anymore."

I hear her hesitate on the other end.

"I can't make it to Syria anymore, Mother," I say, choosing my words slowly. "They will no longer let me come in."

"But you always visit."

"I can't anymore, Mother. They won't let me in." She knows who *they* are. All Syrians do. "I am unwelcome."

Her silence is deafening.

"Can you come for a visit, Mother? I will pay your way."

"Me? I can't go that far."

"I can meet you somewhere, Mother. You don't have to come all the way here. I can meet you somewhere close."

"I can't . . . I can't leave."

"I understand, Mother. Don't worry about it."

"I can't leave. . . . What would I do? . . . What would I wear?"

"Get your ass over here." I crawl, naked. "You're despicable." Jim yanks my head back. He looks straight into my eyes. "You're despicable," he says. He bends down and kisses me. Mouth to mouth. Union.

Cold. Seventh Avenue is crowded. I feel the cold. Damn these American winters.

Bang. Bang. Bang. My brother tries to shoot at some ducks. Misses everything.

I give the duck to my father. He takes it by the neck, bangs its head on a nearby rock. Splat. My mouth drops. Tears start flowing, making streaks along the mud on my face. My father looks at me. Too late. He slaps my face really hard. I can hear my brother smiling way back there.

I came back for my nephew's wedding. He had turned eighteen. He was able to marry a girl from a good family because I paid for the wedding. His mother was happy to see me. My brother was not.

My sister-in-law did not think she was in a position to speak directly to me. She spoke to my mother, who came and told me. My sister-in-law's sister had recently been widowed. She could take care of me, cook for me, clean for me, and bear my children. My mother said I could do better, but the widow was not a bad match. "Do better?" my father spat. "Do you think she would settle for this one after she tried a real man?" He walked away. My mother followed him.

"You're deth-th-th-picable!" Daffy looks at me disdainfully. He is wearing a leather harness and leather chaps cover his skinny legs.

"You're deth-th-th-picable!" He slaps my face hard. "Kith-th-th me, you fool. Gonna fuck your ath-th-th hard."

We sit waiting for my father to finish dinner before we can start. We sit on the ground watching him eat the duck. I am not sure which duck he is eating. But I think I know. He gets up to wash his hands. Before he leaves the room, he smacks me on the back of the head. "You had better eat of this duck," he says. My brother snickers. My mother winces. My hair smells of cooked duck for the rest of my life.

The duck is in the mud. The river rolls along next to it, uncaring. The duck is still alive. It sees me and tries to flee. It can't really move anymore. Helpless. Lonely. I stare at Jim. I start crying.

I was walking along my life, minding my own business, and wham. I don't know what happened. I became a dying man.

I don't feel anything with my fingers anymore. The doctor says I should keep taking the drugs. That sometimes happens the first week and then goes away. Forget it.

Jim stops breathing again. I wonder if this is the real thing.

Keep hope alive. Keep hope alive. What shit.

I force myself to eat a morsel. "You're deth-th-th-picable!" Daffy looks at me disdainfully.

"Stop being so negative," Laura says. "Look at all you've accomplished. You're in your prime. Your whole life's ahead of you. You know, carpe diem and all that."

———

My brother pulls my shorts down. He starts spanking my ass, just like my father. "You're a girl. You're a girl."

I take the DDI once more. The moment I start chewing it, I throw up.

I look at you, my darling, and can't tell who you are.

Where do I put the barrel, under, or over my tongue?

I look at my life and wonder.

Th-th-th-th-that's all, folks.

Fuck.

My Grandmother,
the Grandmaster

I went back to Beirut for my grandmother's eightieth birthday. I am still unsure why I did. Our relationship was tumultuous, but I found myself making plans to visit, after an absence of three years, simply to attend her birthday party. I held back on the gift though. I had still not forgiven what that ornery bitch had said about my last book.

My maternal grandmother, Sitto Nada as we called her, was a large figure in my life. She was a progenitor of large sums of monies paid to my psychiatrists. She treated me like a child, constantly offering advice as well as critiquing what I did. She even criticized my use of the word *progenitor* in the aforementioned sentence, since in her dictionary, it meant "original ancestor." No matter how well thought of a writer I was, I had no right to use words incorrectly, and she sure as hell was not the original ancestor of any monies. She was a strong-willed woman, hated by many, which normally would have endeared her to me, but it was more complicated in this case. She was family.

My mother eloped with my father, fifteen years her senior, when she was fourteen. Sitto Nada, for reasons completely understandable, never forgave my mother for that. Both my maternal grandparents were educated. My grandfather was a physician, a fact Sitto Nada made sure no one ever forgot. She had a bachelor of fine arts degree, which she had earned while married and raising five children. She had married my grandfather at sixteen and wanted something different for her daughters. She had plans for my mother, the youngest of her children, a favorite early on, though by no means as favored as her two sons. Those plans did not include marrying an uneducated peasant living in Africa, no matter how wealthy he was.

My father met my mother at my aunt's wedding in Beirut. My grandparents were living in Jerusalem at the time. The whole family had come to Beirut for the eldest daughter's wedding. My father attended the wedding with relatives. He was visiting from Monrovia, staying for only a couple of weeks. My mother, at thirteen, fell head over heels in love with the dapper gentleman in a turquoise silk suit and fuchsia tie, who openly flirted with her. She loved the mustache. She loved his dark eyes. She even thought the brilliantine looked sexy.

They were of completely different backgrounds. My mother was being taught in the best schools, whereas my father had not been to school since he was nine. That was when he was taken along with his entire family to Liberia. My father started working as a ten-year-old and proved to have the most business sense of all his brothers. By the time he was a young man, he had helped his family amass a sizable fortune.

My grandmother abhorred my father on first sight. She was a good judge of character. It took me years to appreciate her sentiment. She bad-mouthed my father for years to anyone who would listen. Who could blame her? When my mother used to show me old pictures of my father, all I, a young boy of seven or eight, could see was a pimp. He was not a pimp in the traditional sense. He just looked like one, particularly when he smiled. As he always looked into the light for good exposure, his two front gold teeth coruscated, competing for the eyes' attention with the loud ties. Of course, I had heard my grandmother call him a pimp so I knew exactly what the word meant. As he grew older, he toned down his appearance, sublimating his sartorial ostentation to a taste for fancy cars and expensive bric-a-brac.

My grandmother recognized my father's essence without knowing what he told my naïve thirteen-year-old mother as he flirted with her. As God is my witness, this is what he said, as relayed to me by my mother: "Tonight, when I go to the Zeitouneh, I am going to pay a girl to dress just like you so I can fuck her all night thinking it's you." My mother, still unsure what the word *fuck* meant, thought it was incredibly romantic.

Deciding this was the girl he was going to marry, my father drove all the way from Beirut to East Jerusalem to ask her father for his daughter's hand in marriage. My grandfather refused, which must have shocked my father. He was a man used to getting what he wanted. To this day, he still blames my grandmother for the rejection, but I am sure my grandfather hated him just as much.

My grandparents had many reasons to object to the marriage, not the least of which was class difference. Although interclass marriages are fairly common these days, they tended to be rare at the time of my parents' marriage. My mother's family is titled. My father's family is what the titled families, sheikhs and princes, call a peasant family. What it means is that a hundred years ago or more, my mother's family owned the land and my father's family worked it. More so than mere titles, the difference in class was megalithic. My mother's family, particularly her mother's, is one of the oldest Lebanese families. I could name more than ten members on my mother's side, from poets to statesmen, from ruling princes in the fifteenth century to modern ministers, that every Lebanese would recognize. The most famous family member on my father's side was a great-uncle who was dismissed as a shepherd because he was found sodomizing his sheep. Using his camera and a tripod, a Swedish photographer touring the mountains immortalized him committing the act. One could just imagine the dull-witted shepherd so involved in his prurient assignation he did not notice a photographer setting up his equipment.

My father did not take no for an answer. He met my mother as

97

she was coming home from school and asked her to elope with him. She never went home to pack. He drove her to Lebanon, got married in his home village, and took his infant bride to Monrovia the next day. Legally, my grandfather had recourse. In the Druze religion, the girl cannot marry without the consent of her father. My father must have paid a large sum. However, my grandfather did not pursue the matter. The girl was no longer his.

Although my grandparents were always somewhat civil to my father and his family, it was obvious they did not accept them. My father, as much as he hated my grandparents, tried to ingratiate himself with them when they were around. He told his children incredibly vicious stories about my grandmother, never my grandfather. My father called her all kinds of names. He said she was a tyrant. She hated men and had dedicated her life to destroying them. Her father must have paid my grandfather handsomely to take her off his hands because she was so ugly, no decent man wanted to marry her. My father's obsequious behavior did not work on my grandparents. The stories worked on us. All three of us grew up leery of my grandmother.

My father always said my mother did her job. She delivered three boys and no girls for him to worry about. He wanted more, but because of some complications on my way out, the doctor performed a tubal ligation without telling my father. All three of us boys were born in Beirut, in June, each a year apart. My father did not want my mother to deliver in Monrovia, so he planned intercourse around October, for us to be born in summer. That was when the weather in Monrovia was unbearable and my mother had to be in Beirut anyway. He kept doing it in October for a couple of years after I, the youngest, had arrived. It took him a while to figure out my mother was not getting pregnant. The rest of the year, my father had sex with any girl he could get his hands on, but not my mother. She only got October, and then only at first. He stopped when he figured out it was not working. My mother was about twenty-one.

While we were growing up, we spent nine months of the year in Monrovia and the summer in Lebanon. That was fairly typical of Lebanese families in Africa. The man suffered most of the summer heat working while the wife and children left for the cooler climate of the Lebanese mountains. At first we stayed at his family's house in our home village, but then my father decided it was not good enough. I loved that house. It was three hundred years old, walls of huge, yellow ocher and cream stones, and an A-shaped red roof, under which was an attic where all three of us boys played and hid from the evil monsters lurking below. My father built a huge, incredibly ostentatious house right next to the older house, just for the summer months. It had eight bedrooms, ten bathrooms, and six living rooms. The terrace alone was bigger than the entire older house. It was done with exquisite Italian marble, which though aesthetically appealing, was completely inappropriate. We could not run on it when adults were around because it was too precious. When adults were not around, we could not play soccer on it either because the surface was too smooth. We were unable to control the ball. The terrace was utterly useless as far as I was concerned. Everybody in the village thought the house was magnificent. I hated it. It hurt my eyes everywhere I looked, the gold faucets, the crystal chandeliers, the white shag carpet in the sunken living room, the oversize ceramic vases that I could not touch. Daylight lit the house from every angle, and at night floodlights illuminated the entire house, terrace, and gardens, ensuring that no crevice was exposed to the dangers of mystery.

We had to live in it every summer until I was fifteen. My father sold the older family house to our chauffeur. My grandmother never went to our house in the mountains. She called it an abomination.

We never met our grandparents until 1967. Before then, even though they visited Beirut, they never came to visit us, and we were not invited to visit them. When the Israelis invaded all of Palestine in June, my grandparents moved back to Beirut. They settled in a large apartment in Ras Beirut. Once they were back, my mother once again became the complaisant, obsequious daughter. My grandparents allowed us to enter their lives.

The first time we went to visit my grandparents, my mother dressed us all up in our finest clothes. She took us to Red Shoes on Hamra Street to buy new shoes. Mine were black moccasins with gold tassels. I had to wear a tie for the first time. It hurt my neck. I had on a bright green suit, although not with long pants like my brothers, and a yellow shirt.

My mother had spent the entire morning at the hairdresser's. When she did that, I knew she had an important function to attend. She came back with a beehive I had only seen on cans of hairspray. This made me much more nervous. She sat all three of us down, told us how important it was that we behave, how important it was to make a good impression. By the time we got to our grandparents' house, I was perspiring profusely.

When my grandmother opened the door, I thought she was the maid. Only maids opened doors for me. She stood at the door looking at us. She dressed like a maid. She wore a pair of khaki pants and a white shirt. She was the first white-haired woman I had seen. Even poor women dyed their hair in Lebanon. She wore glasses, which accentuated her thick eyebrows. Most amazing of all, she wore no makeup, exactly like maids. She was tall, much taller than I was ever going to get, and thin as a reed. As bad an impression as she made on me, I think we made an ever worse one on her. Her welcoming words were, "Have you lost your eyesight too, Munira? How could you dress them like this?" None of us boys wanted to go in, but my mother had warned us to be on our best behavior. As inauspicious an introduction as it was, we could not back out.

We sat on the living room couch and did not budge for a whole hour. My eyes, on the other hand, took endless walks around the room. It was unlike anything I had ever seen in my life. My grandfather and grandmother ignored me completely. That was fine by me. I was entranced. Every single wall in the room was covered by a huge bookcase. Books in all shapes and sizes, mostly in English, talked to me. In our house, we had a large bookcase, but it was nowhere as big as any of theirs. Ours had no books. We had an *Encyclopaedia Britannica.* My mother always tried to figure how much space to allow between each volume to make sure the bookcase looked full. The rest of it was filled with small pieces of Lalique crystal. My father used to tell me I would be able to tell when I was in a good family's house by noticing how many Lalique crystal ashtrays they had on the table. My grandmother had no Lalique on her table. She did have a stunning chess set. It was obviously something they both used extensively. We had a beautiful chess set at our house, but nobody had figured out how to play the game.

I did not say anything to either of my grandparents on the first visit. I did not say anything the second time either. I was a taciturn child. I was also terrified of my grandmother. I had never met a whore before. That was what my father said she was. The story was fairly well known. My grandmother, while married, fell in love with a French officer during the occupation. They had a torrid affair. Supposedly some patriots were so offended they leaked the name of my grandfather to the French as someone who was fighting the occupation. My grandfather had to escape to Jerusalem, an English colony at the time, and my grandmother was separated from her lover. In later years, when we knew each other well enough to exchange scandals, she dismissed the story. She never denied an affair, just that it was with a Frenchman. She accused the whole race of unhygienic practices. Although I believe the rumors to be wildly apocryphal, I thought her defense a flimsy one. She could force any lover to bathe regularly, if anybody could.

My grandparents had valid reasons for disliking us. First, we looked like my father. I, most of all. We had the dark skin, droopy eyes, and flared Seitounis ears. My father's family, the Seitounis, had intermarried so much, we all looked alike, unfortunately, all rather ugly. The second problem was we were badly brought up, according to my grandmother. We were spoiled (true), snobbish (hard to believe, but true), and not very bright (not true at all). We had pretentious Christian names (Georges, Alex, and Roy), which to this day my father cannot write correctly. My father thought if we had Christian names, as opposed to traditional Lebanese, people would look up to us. The third problem was we had heavy competition. There were a lot of us grandkids, fifteen all together. They all took precedence over us.

Farid was my grandmother's favorite. He was nine years older than I was. Whenever he was around, there was no hope my grandmother would even look at me. Not at first, for he was the eldest son's eldest. He could do nothing wrong. He was named after my grandfather, he wanted to be a doctor, he was beautiful, athletic, and a kiss-ass. Other than that he was basically okay.

In the summer of 1968, everyone in the family, except my father in Monrovia, was invited to my grandmother's house to celebrate my grandfather's sixty-fifth birthday. I was seven years old, the youngest of all the grandchildren. All the kids were downstairs, playing seven stones in the empty lot. The adults tried to get me to go down and play with the others, but I did not want to. I hated the game. It had too much pointless running. You had to pile up the seven stones, then throw a ball at them to disperse them, and then run around, avoiding being hit with the ball, while trying to put the stones back in a pile. I never figured out why you would want to put them back in a pile if you had just hit them. I considered it redundant.

I had squeezed myself in next to my mother, my head barely

reaching the top of the couch's arm. I watched all my aunts and uncles talking about meaningless things. My mother was the best dressed of them all. They all were drinking Turkish coffee from small cups, while I had my glass of orange juice. I would have given anything to have my own cup of coffee.

I kept looking up at the books. Finally, I had the courage to pull one down. I had been looking at the book for a while. I had heard of the title before, the only one in the entire bookshelf. The words on the binding were a siren's call, *The Adventures of Huckleberry Finn*. I knew I could get in trouble for picking it up, but I thought they were all busy and no one would notice. I was right. I was back sitting close to my mother, her smells, the usual comforting elixir. And, I was in love. The book had pictures, which I looked at first. Then, I read the captions. When I was satisfied, I returned to the first page and began to read. The words were difficult at first, but I read them. "You don't know about me without you have read a book by the name of *The Adventures of Tom Sawyer;* but that ain't no matter." I understood it and was proud. I read on: "Tom and me found the money that the robbers hid in the cave, and it made us rich." I had begun an adventure that would last the rest of my life.

Up to that point, I was in love with comics. I would read Superman in English and in Arabic. I read Asterix in French and English. When I was four, I had asked my father to buy a whole collection of Superman comics bound in one volume. He said no, I read too much. He sat me on his lap and explained that reading was okay in small doses, but life was a lot more than just books. I needed to be more active, find alternative diversions, do things that normal boys my age did. I asked him how much money he made in a month. Surprised, he said he made quite a bit. I asked if it was more than $3,000, as large a sum as I could think of. It was in dollars because in Monrovia, my father kept everything in American dollars. He said he made more than that. I then asked him if he made so much, could he not afford to give me three dollars to buy the bound comics? He bought them for me. His harangues on my reading ended not too long after that incident when I discovered he could barely read a newspaper.

I had never read a *real* book before. I felt like an adult, except none of the adults I knew read. I felt like my own person. In later years, I would find this scene with me reading, while everyone around me conversed raucously, to be an interesting allegory of my life. I would grow to find my relationship with books a deeper, more intimate, and more comfortable one than its counterpoint with people. As Sitto Nada wrote when she read my last book, I had become a misanthropic writer, an accurate description, but not what one would expect from one's grandmother.

"The widow she cried over me, and called me a poor lost lamb, and she called me a lot of other names, too, but she never meant no harm by it." The book talked to me. Unfortunately, it was not the only one. "Roy," my grandmother called. I looked up and noticed the whole room was quiet. She must have been calling me for a while. I had not heard.

"Are you reading the book, Roy?" she asked in a gentle voice. This was the first time I recalled her addressing me personally. I nodded, scared, not sure what the correct response was. Everybody, it seemed, was looking at me.

"Do you understand what you are reading?"

I nodded again and moved even closer to my mother.

"I'm sure he does," my mother said, coming to my rescue. "Roy can read in three languages. He's already skipped a class." I kept nodding. They should talk about someone else.

"Come sit next to me," Sitto Nada said, patting the seat next to her. I shook my head. I did not want to be near her. "Come on," she continued. "Don't be shy. Come sit next to me." I kept shaking my head and tried going in between my mother's back and the backseat of the couch. My mother was whispering and cajoling, "Go sit next to your grandmother." I kept shaking my head. My mother pleaded in my ear. I felt she was betraying me.

"If you come over here," Sitto Nada said, "I will tell you how they found the money in the cave." That stopped my shaking head. I looked at my grandmother. She was smiling. If she smiled more often, people would not think she was a whore, I thought. I hesitated. She pointed at all the books around the room. She switched to English and in a perfect accent said, "If you come here and show me you can read the book, I will give it to you. I might even give you another one when you're done with this." I was sitting next to her in a flash. I heard my grandfather laughing, saying something about finding matches.

We sat close. I did not mind her smells. Her arm draped my shoulders. I felt secure. The room reverted to its habitual palaver. My grandmother and I cocooned with Huck. She asked me to read to her. She was surprised at my skill. "You do know it is written in incorrect English," she said, still in English, as if testing me. "That kind of English is called slang."

"Yes," I said, looking up at her from my book, "they're black. All black people speak like that."

What followed was the first of many lectures. Tom and Huck were not black. Not all black people spoke like that. Not all black people were our servants. She spoke of worlds completely different from mine at the time. In my world, all blacks worked for us and they all spoke incorrect English. She endeavored to explain the difference between slang and dialect.

I ended up going home with Tom and Huck, on the condition that I come back the following week, alone, and tell her everything I had read. It became a weekly event. I read many books that summer. The second book was R. D. Blackmore's *Lorna Doone.* I wish I could remember the rest of the books she gave me. Once she took me in, I found in her a friend unlike anybody else. I rarely talked to anybody, but with her, I would never shut up. I told her stories about me, about my father, about life in Africa. She told me stories of Jerusalem, and of colonial times. We would tell each other about the books we had read. I began to make up stories, as if I read them in a book, about war heroes fighting ogres. There were damsels in distress who ended up as dinner for the hunters who killed the dragon. There was the child who was swallowed whole by a lion, only to grow in its belly and become the lion king. "And you read that in this book?" she would ask. Yes, yes, I would say and come up with an even more implausible story.

In 1970, my father sent his three boys to Beirut to live with his sister. He decided education in Monrovia was atrocious. The schools were much better in Beirut. I was almost ten when school started. I was enrolled at a school called International College, the best school in Lebanon. My brothers did not pass the entrance exam and were in a different school. I believe my passing that exam was the beginning of my father's feelings of inadequacy towards me, which I helped to foster later on, of course.

My school was in Ras Beirut, close to my grandmother's apartment. She told me I was to come over every Wednesday for lunch. I agreed wholeheartedly, even though I was to find out she was not a very good cook. She had asked me what kind of food I liked and I said chicken. For three years, every Wednesday, I had chicken. Never failed. Chicken with thyme, chicken with pine nuts, chicken with rice, chicken with tomato, you name it. These days, I can honestly say, I do not eat chicken. I hate it. Not only was my grandmother's cooking one-dimensional, she used no salt because of my grandfather's heart problems. She continued without salt even after he died in 1972.

Nevertheless, when Wednesday noon arrived, and we broke from class, I ran to see her. We had this ritual. I would return the book I had borrowed from her. I took another one. Then I would sit for lunch across the table from her—my grandfather would sit at the head of the table reading his paper—and we would play chess, or really, she would teach me chess.

My grandmother played chess. Not the way normal people played chess. She played the game. It was her one true passion. In the beginning, she would teach me how each piece moved. By the time I picked that up, she began teaching me openings. At the age of ten, I could discuss advanced strategies with her. I was not very good and was probably a disappointment to her. I could hold my own. I used to beat everybody in my age group, but we both knew that was not enough. We had to be better than an invisible opponent we both had, someone who was good enough to understand the beauty of the ultimate game. The opponent could not be found in Lebanon. My grandmother could beat hers. I could not beat mine.

She was so good she played chess by mail. She would send her moves to all the different players around the world, one move every couple of weeks. Games took forever. I remember one game she played against Bocsic, a Yugoslavian grandmaster. He had written a paper on the superiority of the Sicilian Defense. She had white and allowed him to play his favorite defense, just to show him how wrong he was. She beat him. She even played an Israeli grandmaster (three draws in a row), putting aside political beliefs for the sake of the game. They had to send their mail through a French intermediary in Paris. She explained to me the intricacies of the Queen's Gambit and the Queen's Gambit Declined. I had to study all of Alekhine's and Capablanca's moves. She recognized Fischer's genius before he became a household name, long before he beat Spassky for the world title.

She was a grandmaster. She was never crowned such since she never played in a sanctioned tournament. The Lebanese chess federations were disorganized and, according to my grandmother, unashamedly misogynous. I was to find out later that it was not only the Lebanese organizations that were misogynous. None of the men she played with, grandmasters or not, believed it was a woman on the other side. They assumed it was another male grandmaster playing a trick on them.

In October of 1971, it was announced at my school that a young Russian grandmaster was coming to Lebanon. He was to play forty-five games at the same time with students. It was a promotion of some kind, which my grandmother found patently offensive. She saw it as an insult to the great game. At first, she did not want me to be involved. I was the first of the forty-five to be picked, of course. My game, although nowhere near as good as my grandmother's or where we both thought it should be, was still better than that of anybody else at school. She then changed her mind and decided to accompany me to the event.

The chess event was held in a large hall at school. All the kids were placed on three long tables, at right angles, facing the podium. The accompanying parents were seated behind their child. We each had a chess set placed in front of us. My grandmother sat right behind me. When I noticed I had black for my game, I looked back at her, complaining about my luck.

"Don't worry," she said. "We're going to cut off this fake grandmaster's balls."

My jaw dropped. I had never heard that kind of language from a woman before. She winked at me, and I could not stop laughing. My nervousness evaporated. I was ready for the future ball-less wonder.

The headmaster, an American from Minnesota, gave a long speech about the importance of chess in a man's life (not a woman's). He thanked the Russian grandmaster. The latter was surprisingly young, in his early thirties. He had dark hair and dark eyes.

He looked aloof, arrogant, and contemptuous. I thought he should not feel so superior wearing those cheap plaid pants. The headmaster told us what an honor it was to have a champion play us, mere mortals. I felt my grandmother bristle and I began to get angry. I wanted the soon-to-be-castrato to come down from the podium and play.

As the school's best chess player, I was seated right in the middle, twenty-two students on each side of me. The headmaster asked all the boys playing white to make their first move. The Russian came down from the podium and began to play each game. He moved clockwise. At my game, he opened with a normal pawn to king four and walked over to play the next player. He averaged about ten minutes before he came back around to me again, at first because he was playing straight openings, and then, when the middle games were in progress, because there were fewer of us left. I played a straightforward Ruy Lopez. We were fairly even until my grandmother took over. I wanted to defend a pawn when I heard, "No." I did not look back at first. I tried to figure out what she wanted me to play. I tried moving my rook, to solidify the defense, and the same "No" was uttered. She wanted me to come out with my queen. She wanted nothing to do with a safe game. When the Russian arrived, he shook his head in mockery, began attacking my pawn, and moved on.

"Just remember, Roy," she said calmly, "what did Emily Brontë say in *Wuthering Heights*? Proud people breed sad sorrows for themselves. Let's hit him over the head with his sorrows, shall we?"

I was having a grand old time. I knew my grandmother could trounce this pretender in any game. She took over completely. He would come around, move his piece, and leave. She would dictate the response. He began to slow down at our game. I say *our*, and not *her*, because technically I was sitting in front of the board. I could tell he was slightly confused when he got to me. I developed this pose. I sat on my hands, looking up at him, and smiled from ear to ear, about to laugh hysterically. The minute he moved, I giggled. Everybody looked at me strangely, but I was having too good a time to care. Soon, he was left with only our game. He had won all the rest. By that time, we had won and he should have resigned. He thought he could save the game against an amateur like me. It was now one-on-one.

He made his move. I was giggling. Sitto Nada had already prepared me. "Mate in seven," I said in English. His eyes grew wide.

"Five," my grandmother said to me. "Five, not seven."

"Mate in five," I chirped. I still looked at him with a smile that would not stop. He now looked at my grandmother with venomous eyes. He thought he could intimidate her, the fool.

He called the translator over and said something to him in Russian. Sitto Nada smiled and said something back to him in Russian. The pretender's face reddened. He violently picked up the chessboard and threw it away. He walked off in a huff. The head of the Lebanese chess federation came at us as if to scream. My grandmother stood up, and he cowered. I could not stop laughing. It was such fun. The hall was in chaos, but all I could do was keep tugging at her skirt to get her attention. I wanted to find out what she had said.

We walked back to her apartment hand in hand. I did not know she spoke Russian. She said she spoke Arabic, French, English, Russian, and German. I was so proud of her. I tried to find out what she had told him. She said she had only responded to what he had said, refusing to elaborate more. He had told the translator to tell the old hag not to play the little boy's game. If she wanted to play, he could find some other old hag to play her. I jumped up and down beside her, begging her to tell me what she had said. She refused. Finally I asked, "Do you know how to say *balls* in Russian?"

"I sure do," she said. We laughed all the way back.

My grandfather died, a year later, in October of 1972. He had a quick heart attack. It came suddenly without any warning. He was sitting in his favorite chair, reading one of his newspapers, keeled over, and died. For some reason, the person most affected by his death was my mother. One of her sisters called her in Monrovia and told her to come to Beirut because their father was sick. Her sister did not want to tell her he was dead over the phone. My mother arrived and collapsed the minute she found out the truth. She did not stop crying for three whole days. My mother never went back to Monrovia to live after that. She bought her own apartment in Beirut and we lived with her.

My grandmother was stoic at the funeral, almost Northern European. She did not shed a tear. She accepted the condolences with dignity. People talked about her insensitivity, her cruelty. She paid it no heed. She would not lose her composure till later, till a war took away the last vestiges of her dignity.

She lived on, missing my grandfather for sure, but our routine did not change for a while. I still had lunch at her place every Wednesday.

It did change, however. A year later, in 1973, Farid's father, her eldest son, had a quarrel with my father, which turned into a feud. My father had gone into a business venture with my uncle and it went sour. They both lost quite a bit of money, but for obvious reasons, it meant a lot more to my uncle. My father thought my uncle was overreacting. My uncle considered that an insult. He decided that no one in his family was to speak to anyone in ours. Since he was the eldest son, and my grandfather was no longer among the living, he felt it was his mother's duty not to talk to us. I assume she argued, but he gave her an ultimatum. She had to either cut off our family or his. If she spoke to us, he would forbid his family to speak to her.

I always considered the decision for her was between Farid and me. She chose Farid. I was devastated. I never recovered. I was left floundering. My mother was the one to tell me I was no longer welcome on Wednesdays, no chicken for lunch. She sat me down one morning, explaining that Sitto Nada could not talk to me anymore. Words made no sense. The world made no sense. I was left with nothing to hold on to.

There are decisions in life that are irreversible. By the time the war started and I was in the United States, my grandmother had gotten her son to talk to my mother. They got together and commiserated about my father being a charlatan, a mountebank. My grandmother wrote me constant letters, some apologetic, some didactic. I told her I forgave her, but it was never the same again. She was too proud to beg forgiveness, and I was too proud to accept anything less. Proud people breed sad sorrows for themselves.

The only time I felt close to her again was on my first trip back to Beirut. The Murabitoun, a now defunct Sunni militia, had ransacked her apartment. They broke into her home while she was in the shelter below, stole nothing, but destroyed every valuable thing in the place. They tore the curtains, burned her fox coat in the middle of the Persian rug. They tore up her books and broke her favorite chess set. All for no apparent reason.

She came to welcome me back. We were sitting at my mother's kitchen table, away from everybody else. She told me what had happened to her place. She started crying.

"They destroyed everything," she said between sobs, "everything. Someone defecated on my dining room table. Right smack in the middle. They didn't take anything. I would have felt better if they did. But, nothing. They took nothing. They just wanted to destroy my life. They broke every single piece of my chess set, not just the set. Someone went to all the trouble of breaking each piece one by one. I can't believe someone would do this."

I was so moved. I reached for her hand. I could only imagine what would have happened to me if someone had come into my place and torn up my books. She pulled her hand away, taking out a broken watch she kept in her brassiere.

"This is your grandfather's watch," she said. "They took it out of my nightstand and stepped on it till it broke. I don't understand why they didn't take it. It's valuable. They could sell it. Someone could wear it. Why destroy it? Why destroy something that means so much to someone? Why?"

We move on with our lives. Different things become important. My writing became the most important thing in my life. Beirut, and its memories, began to recede to the background. I was able to re-build my grandmother's library by sending her boxes and boxes of books.

My father disinherited me. He did not approve of the subject of my books. My mother left him. He gave her a million dollars and kept the rest. She felt that was an insult and developed chronic cases of neuralgia. She spent about a year in bed with hot-water bottles. My mother cursed her husband. She told him God would revenge her indignity. My father was rich enough to have dispensed with God. His fortune went downhill, though, years later with the civil war in Liberia. It was unexpected. He was a good businessman, but completely unaware of political situations. At the first sign of chaos in Monrovia, the Liberians attacked any property or business owned by Lebanese. All the Lebanese were then officially deported and their properties confiscated. My father still had enough to live on comfortably, but lost enough to make my mother happy.

My brother Georges does not talk to me. My brother Alex does. My mother says she loves me, but cannot begin to fathom who I am.

My grandmother writes me a letter a week. I reply less often, but I do reply. In her letters, she actually has the gumption to cri-tique my writing. I keep telling her she goes too far, but it does not change. When I show her letters to my editor, who celebrated her eightieth birthday a week after my grandmother, she gets apoplectic. She tells me my grandmother is crazy, obnoxious, and would not know good writing from her sphincter muscle. Of course, my grandmother's criticisms of my writings and books include comments on the terrible editing my work receives. Finally, I got them to write directly to each other. It seems to be working. They insult each other in between recipe exchanges and book reviews. My grandmother is kind when it comes to other people's books.

She met Spassky in Geneva and Karpov in Paris. She convinced both to have a game with her. How she did that is beyond me. She lost both games. She wrote them down and sent them to me.

She is coming over to visit next year. She is the only member of my family who has ever visited me. She is the only member of my family who has met my lover. She keeps trying.

Sometimes, I wish I were less proud.

Whore

A breeze flirts under my skirt. The light is silver, a little violet as the darker clouds begin to triumph. A cold, January morning and I am late. I had to park my car a distance away as the early mourners had beaten me to the best spots. I walk up the hill, carrying my coat in the crook of my arm.

It will probably rain. Another possible disaster to consider. It is not cold enough for snow today. The olive grove is above me, above the oaks, above the house. The fig trees above the olives, the peach trees above the figs, the apples, the cherries, all in order. Tears well up in my eyes, but do not drop. I hope it is an omen for the weather. Those trees call forth memories. I am no longer a child.

Beirut spreads behind me. Interminable, a sprawling, disheveled city of mottled, self-conscious buildings. I remember so much. Capacious memory. From the house, I can see Beirut. I can see the azure of the Mediterranean, the tides, the flux, the struggle of a town in bloom against its web, *contre la mer, contre la mère.* The city sheds its shackles only to find that chains held its soul.

I can see beauty. The house changed. I grew up. Beirut changed. It regressed. The scene changed. They built hideosities on the mountain, calling them buildings, selling them for outrageous sums to families unable to afford the more outrageous sums a flat in Beirut went for. And my father's funeral is today.

When I was young, my father would call the family to come see the sunset. We would sit on the terrace ledge and watch, my father, my mother, my four sisters. We always sat in order, for we were an orderly family in spite of the alleged artistic talent; father, mother, Yasmine, me, May, Ghada, Hind. We looked at Beirut, at the golden Mediterranean, at the horizon. The yellow transmutes, a bar of blood, a stain of orange, a threat of green. I looked, I saw, but I did not see what my father, the artist, saw. I wondered for a long time why I never saw what others did. Could they not see the smear of crimson across the membrane of the sky? Could they not see the violence? My father stood and explained the sunset. He was the alleged master of the watercolor sunset. I tried hard to understand what he was saying. I try. I want to respect him. I want to understand what he sees.

He bemoaned the fact he had no son he could teach to become an artist, to pass the mantle to. My mother looked at her feet, my sisters quivered restlessly, I was busy with color explosions. He had no son. He suffered; aesthetics rejoiced.

I sat on the terrace ledge endlessly, even when my father stopped. He did not want to see his beloved city in flames. I did. It was exquisitely sumptuous. The rockets, the shells, the flares, all painted the empty canvas in my head. Guns ejaculated blood. Cannons coruscated at night like flickers of diamonds. He lived for beauty, he said. What did I live for? I spent hours meditating on what I lived for. He kept talking about beauty. I wanted to see as he did. I looked, I stared, but I saw none. I wondered what was wrong with me. They bought his cheap paintings. Everyone must have believed in beauty I never saw.

I walk up the hill, catching up with a group of mourners from a neighboring village, mostly *ajaweed,* the religious Druze. The men and women begin to separate. I check my dress, all black, my head kerchiefed, transparent white muslin, traditional mourning wear. I walk behind the women. The men move towards the oaks, where the males sit under a large canvas strung across the trees. The few family men stand up. The arriving mourners stand next to each other in front of the family. The mourners are disorganized at first, but the leader, a potato-nosed old man in a white beard and ancestral Druze dress, takes charge. "Like the old days," he says. "We stand like the old days. Keep the old traditions." He looks withered, desiccated.

All together, "May He bless you this morning."
    "May He bless you this morning," the family men reply.
    "May you be compensated for with your health."
    "And with your health, if Allah so pleases."
    The mourners come to kiss the family men, in line, the eldest first. Words of condolence echo privately. The mourners then move and sit with friends. The family men sit. They wait for the next batch.

The women shout greetings to the men: "May you be compensated for with your health." Some of the men reply. The women keep moving to the house. To my mother's house, not mine. I nod to the family members on my left. They all acknowledge. Some begin whispering while I can still see them. Discretion and subtlety were the first casualties of the civil war. It seems so long ago. Only Zouzou smiles at me and waves discreetly. I berate myself for being late.

The oaks were where I used to play. They are the center of the village. The children gathered there. The boys ganged up on my cousin until I showed up. The rest of the tribe, my sisters and my cousins, would feel guilty and stand by Zouzou and me against the village. Am I still protecting him or is it the other way round?

Zouzou and I are almost the same age. He gave me a chance to witness what it was like on the other side. As a young boy, he was unable to keep his hands off his penis. Day or night, fully dressed or in his pajamas, his hand would unconsciously drop and feel his treasure. To make sure it was still there, or it felt good, I was never completely sure. I just found it amusing. On a limpid summer day, more than twenty-five years ago, I climbed the mulberry tree. I was an expert at picking the juicy berries, dark purple, almost black. I shared my bounty with everyone. I watched hands and mouths color. Zouzou's face was all purple. I looked down and giggled. His white shorts had a reddish spot encircling his penis, exactly the size of his hand. His mother arrived to share in the mulberries. She screamed at Zouzou for soiling his shorts. She could not figure how he got mulberry juice down there.

I grew up among these oaks. Even though my father could afford a house in Beirut. We were year-rounders. My uncle's family was not. At the beginning of the summer, when they moved in next door, I was the first to greet them. Zouzou's face lit up behind the car window when he saw me. Beirut may have been only twenty-five minutes away, but it was worlds apart. We would sit together, making fun of all the villagers as they came to greet his parents. Family after family, we knew all their secrets. Since my uncle and father were important, but not titled, everybody came to visit, not just the men. We would sit at the top of the stairs, watching the families chatter endlessly, saying the same things they had said the year before and the year before that. Meaningless, endlessly revolving, insincere conversations. Nothing changed.

The titled family of the village had their own house. It stood aloof on its hill. I considered it the most beautiful thing I had ever seen. I have been in it only once. It stood empty most of the year, mirroring my loneliness. In June, the house lit up. The entire male population of the village gathered under the oaks for the welcoming pilgrimage. Zouzou was allowed to go, but I was not. I wondered what went on in there. At one point, Yasmine became friends with their daughter. My mother was so proud. My mother sang their praises. Yasmine would learn class. I was invited to the house, never to return because I had the audacity to touch voluptuous things. My mother apologized for me. She told them she had no idea what to do with me.

At the end of the summer, they returned the visits. The titled family went to every house in the village. They visited our house last, for the head always bought paintings from my father before he went down to Beirut. My father, ever obsequious, would almost prostrate himself in front of the head, flamboyant, unabashed sycophancy. He practically gave away his paintings. When the head walked in, my father would use the traditional submissive handshake, shake with the right and use the left hand to cover as well. The head's one hand was worth two of my father's. My mother cooked up a storm and tried to entertain the head's wife, who always seemed bored, always sickly. The head's wife looked experienced in ill health. Then they left and everything went back to normal.

I arrive at the house with the women. The rituals are less rigid. The family women stand to greet the mourners. The coffin is in the middle of the room. Black, white, and bad blond dyes dominate. My mother is the first to embrace me, her kiss as dry as chalk. She cries. "Traffic," I lie.

"I don't know how I'm going to go through this," she tells me. All I can see is her hair, lustrous black through the white muslin. "I'm scared."

"It's going to be okay, Mama." I know it is not. "I'll be beside you."

"Can you spend the night? Just tonight, please. I don't want to be alone tonight. I don't want to ask any of your sisters."

"Sure. Tonight. I can be here tonight." I, the family spinster, expect this. I had put away my paints before I came up.

"Can you check on Hind? She's in my room. She's been in there for a while. I wonder if something is wrong."

"I will," I say. "Just give me a minute to go through the line."

Yasmine hugs me. My aunt kisses. She wears lipstick. I feel her mustache. May kisses me and mentions my tardiness. Ghada notices my skirt is not buttoned correctly. The wind could blow right through it. Didn't I notice? she asks. I nod at the rest of the family. My aunts, my cousins, my relatives, my acquaintances.

I excuse myself, walking the never quite familiar labyrinth to the bedrooms. I stifle the urge to open the door to my own bedroom. There will be enough time for nostalgia. I walk into my mother's room, fixing my skirt's buttons as I close the door behind me. Hind sits on the bed weeping. The ubiquitous bottle of Lexotanil, her favorite tranquilizer, is by her side.

"Where have you been?" she asks angrily.

"Late. Are you okay?"

"No, I'm not okay. How can I be okay? How can you ask such a question?" A few more hysterical sobs.

"How many have you taken?"

"None of your business. It helps me relax."

I figure the relationship changed on her wedding night six months ago. A switch went on. I was her favorite sister. She got married. I became the unmarried one.

God is wicked, a trickster. My uncle had four boys. The youngest two days older than Hind. When he was born, I got desserts and rose water. Two days later, all I saw were tears. I was upset. One more to help with household chores was not a good compensation.

I taught Hind. I spent time with her. I expanded possibilities. I instructed her on different strokes to swim against the current. I deluded myself again. I failed. She sits before me a younger replica of my sisters.

I sit next to her and let her cry. I look at my father's painting on the wall. A pallid watercolor of a mountain village with the omnipresent sheep. He loved his sheep. He loved his viridian, and his yellow ocher; dab, dab, pat, pat, pat, comma stroke, comma stroke, reverse comma stroke, check-mark stroke, dab, pat, dab. There you are, darling. That's how you paint a mountain range. Do you want me to do it again for you?

What is the secret?

I notice eyeglasses on his nightstand. I am surprised to see a couple of monographs, Corot and Constable. Maybe he was stuck on the letter C. I wonder if he ever looked at them. My hands desperately want to touch. My eyes want to feast. I have to control myself. This is not the time. I move the newspaper of three days ago to cover the books. There are at least ten bottles of pills: heart, high blood pressure, and tranquilizers.

"Is Mama okay?" she asks me.

"Yes. She's wondering about you. Are you ready to come out?"

"I need to see Kamal. Do you think I could call him? Did you see him when you were coming up? Is he okay?"

"Your husband is fine. Don't worry about him."

"I'm sorry I shouted at you."

"That's quite all right," I say. Ten years younger than me, but a higher status it seems.

"You should take a pill. It helps you relax. You're probably the only one without anything. But then again, you always were the strong one." *Strong*, in my family's language, means insensitive, unfeeling, and harsh. She stands, stuffing her accessories in her handbag. I realize I forgot mine. She gives me her hand to help me stand up. She looks at my hand and notices a spot of cobalt blue.

"Were you painting?" she yells at me.

"Were you breathing?" I snap back.

She walks ahead of me, shaking her head. "I can't believe you were painting on the day of your father's funeral."

I sit between my mother and May. Ghada is on my mother's other side. She wails. I wonder how long before the professionals start. My mother's eyes do not stray from the coffin in front of her.

"How could you leave us orphaned?" Ghada screams at the coffin. "How can I live without you?" She unconsciously adjusts her skirt, to make sure it covers her knees, as if my father were still in the room. He used to look at my mother or any one of us, and we would all adjust our skirts. We could not show anything above the knees.

Women cry around me. Tears continue to well up in my eyes, but to no avail.

"I'm an orphan now," May joins in. She is the most successful of us all. She married our first cousin Akram, a very rich man now, after the war. Her black Escada dress shows it. Her heaving bust fascinates me. Akram paid for silicone implants. I note how natural they bounce as she sobs. He also paid for liposuction as well as some tucks around her eyes. At thirty-five, she now looks exactly her age.

At thirty-five my mother had five girls. She had Yasmine at nineteen, me at twenty, May at twenty-one, a miscarriage, Ghada at twenty-four, two miscarriages, Hind at thirty, and one more miscarriage. My father always thought the miscarriages were boys. He believed he was paying for some sin he had committed. My mother became a grandmother at forty-two. Yasmine had a girl. Boys were later born to Yasmine, May, and Ghada, but they did not have my father's name.

A woman I recognized from the neighboring village yells, "Oh, my God. Oh, my God." It is coming from the back, but I don't look. Tears roll down my mother's cheeks. My aunt stands up and walks to the coffin. She drapes herself across it. Her blond hair is what I notice, as well as her vestigial, black mustache. "Oh, my brother," she wails, elongating her words. She keeps repeating, "Oh, my brother." A mantra, but melodious, it begins to sound like a song. I want to tap my foot. Ghada stands up and leads her aunt back to her chair.

"I hate her," May whispers to me, speaking of our bereft aunt. "I really hate her. It's just drama. She's always so dramatic at funerals."

I nod. I do not know what to say. More mourners come in to save me. I stand up. One of the women is our hairdresser. Ghada breaks down as she hugs her. "He's dead," she tells her coiffeuse. "He's dead." The coiffeuse strokes my sister's hair.

The head's wife walks in. My mother stands up automatically. A trace of a smile graces her face. She cannot help herself. Toadying, she seats the head's wife next to her in Ghada's seat. The head's wife looks as pallid as ever, her skin almost sheer, pellucid, her porous nose a light gray. She is family now, though.

Images abound. The dining table has been moved to accommodate the mourners. The seven of us sat around it. The girls giggled as my father lost his hair before our eyes. "Look, Mama," he said as hair came off in his hand. "My hair is deserting me. I will be bald in no time." My mother told him he would always be handsome to her. Yasmine said bald men were distinguished. He smiled at her. I tried to say something. I wanted to make him feel all right. "You still have your painting."

My mother leans across to talk to May. "Are they going to do traditional prayers?"

"Yes, Mama," May replies. "Akram handled it."

"How? I thought they were not going to budge. I thought the traditional sheikhs refused to pray."

"They will, Mama. They will. Don't worry about it. Papa would not have wanted modern prayers. He's going to get traditional prayers. I promise."

"They will all pray?"

"They will all pray, Mama, all of them."

I wait a couple of seconds to ask May what is going on.

"They were not going to pray for him," she tells me. This is the first I have heard of this.

"Who?"

"Those bastard sheikhs."

"Why not?"

"Because Ghada married a Shiite."

"Oh, dear."

"Can you believe that? Some people are still living in the dark ages." May's breasts still fascinate me.

"How did Akram handle it?"

"He paid them, of course. How else does he handle anything? All they fucking wanted was money. Two hundred dollars. That was all it took to buy the whole lot of them. They did not want Lebanese pounds. They wanted dollars. Two hundred dollars and they will pray for your soul. Piety is sure cheap these days."

I nod.

I spend some time behind my eyelids. Thinking, remembering, attempting to configure my feelings. I cannot move. My father is dead, the primary motivator in my life dissolved. I wonder how it is possible. My father, a thorn in my side, a rose in my heart. No tears flow for roses yet. I wonder if I am defective.

I remember the day of ecstasy, what would have been the happiest day of my life. On a boat, with my father and uncle, Yasmine and my cousins. I found the powerboat exhilarating. Everybody wanted to fish. I wanted the boat to keep moving. At the end of the day, as they steered it home, I stood up, intoxicated by a sense of freedom, of pure joy, of sensuality. My face must have looked so impassioned, my father screamed. The motor, the sea spray, all conspired against him. I only heard him when his face was right in front of mine, livid. I went too far. I scared him. I began to realize that any expression of passion was to be avoided at any cost when he was around. Rapture terrifies.

———

One spring, Zouzou's father bought a lamb, a young, beautiful animal with whom all of us fell in love. We raised it in our house, but it truly was Zouzou's lamb. My father warned us. Don't get attached to it, he said, for it would be a grand meal in a few months. We did not listen. We called him Darrin, like the husband on *Bewitched*. Zouzou fed him, Ghada played with him, and Hind dressed him up in old clothing. May took him on walks in the village, and I gave him a pink froufrou with food coloring. Even though we were warned, we still felt betrayed when my uncle took Darrin to the butcher. Zouzou could not openly cry so he locked himself in his room. Hind wailed for hours. Even Yasmine could not contain her tears. Nonetheless, we all had to sit at the table when Darrin was served. My father and mother ate. My uncle and aunt ate. We could not. No amount of cajoling could get us, the children, to try a morsel.

Later, alone, while the afternoon napped, I stole into the kitchen and served myself a plate of Darrin over rice, with pine nuts. I ate voraciously, savoring each bite, with my fingers, licking everything clean.

The wailers commence. These women are very good. "The mountains will never be the same without you." My mother cries uncontrollably. "You had a wonderful wife." They all cry. "You raised an exemplary family." Yasmine is in hysterics. She looks at me, the strong one, and puts out her hand. She needs me. I go over and hug her as she cries and cries. She was his favorite. I love her for it. It is Hind's turn to drape herself across the coffin. "Who will paint your pictures?" My hackles involuntarily rise. "What is life without you?"

My father was proud of my first painting. His corny first words stuck: "Not bad for a little girl." As I explored, my paintings became bad for any girl, for any human. When I sold my first painting, he was beside himself. When I sold a painting for more money than he ever sold any of his, he was incensed; *apoplectic* was the word I would use. He told me he was the better artist. I was a pretender. He told me he was more famous than I will ever be. I agreed with him. He asked me to stop painting. I wondered how he could ask such a thing. Can I stop my life? He never saw what I was seeing. I wanted him to. I wanted him to look at my paintings. I wanted him to see, just to see.

I was such a disappointment.

En plein air. I walked in on my mother. She worked on her latest Aubusson, another Palestinian-patterned cross-stitch count. I asked where my father was. "He is painting *en plein air*. You can see him right behind the cypress." I found him. Imitating his heroes, he wore a beret and his painting coat. In terms of looking like a painter, Monet had nothing on him.

"Go back and bring the other easel," he said. "You can paint this beautiful scene." Gesturing, in large arm movements, he included everything from the hills to the sea to the cityscape. Yet, he only painted one small hill. "You can learn a lot if you go back to nature. That is what it's all about. Go back and don't forget to bring a canvas. It'll be good for you to try painting small."

I came back and set myself behind him. Was I afraid of him looking? Within minutes the brush moved of its own free will. Damn perspective, Beirut sat on top of the mountains, under the sea. I looked at my father. He worked on a tree's shadow in the left corner. My brush moved. Alone, betraying me, while I was looking at him, the brush included him in the painting. From a small figure, the brush decided to make him overpowering. Bigger and bigger, he grew. Instead of his own brush, he held a lightning bolt. He stood atop the city, atop the mountains, owning it all. My sky grew darker, stormy. The brush kept moving.

"What are you doing?"

"I'm painting," I said, stunned.

"What kind of painting is that?" He was angry again. "How could you get *that* painting from this wonderful scene?"

"I don't know."

"Can't you just look? How can you look at something so beautiful and make that? Why did you have to bring Zeus into this? Why do you have to complicate everything? Can't you paint something peaceful?"

"I don't know."

"Your colors are all wrong anyway."

Why was I unable to show him?

"What is life without you?" my aunt wails. I wonder.

Yasmine is calmer. "I need a cigarette," she tells me. Everyone is smoking inside, but she wants to go out. We walk out together, climb up a bit to the olive grove. She offers me a cigarette since mine are in my orphaned handbag. I can see the family burial grounds from up here. Not long before he is in there, interred with his forefathers, buried somewhere deep within me.

"Ghada is driving me crazy," she tells me.

"Why?" I ask, because it is my turn.

"She pretends she is the only one who loved him. She's the one suffering the most. She always wants to be the center of attention."

"It's just the way she is." When did I become the peacemaker?

Yasmine pops a Valium. "I need a cup of coffee."

"Why aren't we serving any?"

"Nobody serves anything at burials. It would be disgraceful. You should know that, Rana. You really ought to do your duties. You should attend funerals. You can't live so isolated from everything. It's not right."

Rain has not yet come. It is getting colder. Maybe it will snow, which is easier to handle than rain. Two women walk out the front door for a smoke. They do not see us above them.

"It's so sad," the first one says. They are familiar, but I can't place them. From the dresses, you can tell they are Beirutis, not village women, more modern.

"He was such a great artist," the second one says.

"The poor thing. Five girls, you know it's her fault." The woman speaks, yet she looks rigid, unmalleable. Her lapidary features, her height, and her arid demeanor suggest lifelessness, torpor.

Yasmine tenses up. She is about to say something, but I hold her back. I am intrigued.

"Did you notice May? She is so beautiful."

"Yes, but not as beautiful as the second one, Rana, the unmarried one." It feels strange hearing them talk about me.

"She is beautiful, but she's a whore. She killed him." Yasmine bristles, but I am calm. I shush her. I want to hear this.

"She's a whore? I thought she's a lesbian. Doesn't she have a lover?"

"She does. It's her cousin Zouzou. He sleeps at her apartment all the time."

"She has her own apartment? That's strange."

"She's lived alone for ten years. She was twenty-six when she moved out. It drove her father crazy. She killed him. He hated her. He hated her paintings. She blackened his name, the poor thing."

"Well, I hate to admit it. She may be a whore, but I love her paintings. I saw one the other day and I thought it was so unbelievably beautiful."

I hear myself say, not me really, but possibly some trickster ventriloquist using me as the medium, "Thank you. That's very kind of you."

The women looked up at us, shocked. They hesitate, not knowing what to do or say. They stamp out their cigarettes and walk backward into the house. Yasmine is confused by my reaction. I smile.

The room is white. My father's paintings hang on every wall. A hundred women or more sit quietly, some weeping silently. The wailers have stopped. The calm before the storm; the lull before the cacophony. I sit between my mother and my aunt. I notice Yasmine holding Ghada's hand. We all know what is coming.

I wait for the deluge.

The poet begins his elegy. His voice carries clearly from the oaks. He sings of my father as my family cries. "You who made the mountains proud." The men sing some verses with him. "You, the head of your illustrious family." The women wail in harmony. "You who have immortalized our homes." He rhymes his verse as the pain in my heart swells. "Even though you had no boy to cry 'Daddy,' you had five daughters whose eyes shone like stars." He repeats the damn couplet as the pain gets unbearable. I am furious. A wail comes from somewhere within me, somewhere I do not know. My tears gush out, a veritable waterfall. I cry uncontrollably. My hand instinctively reaches out to the coffin. I do not recognize myself. I am possessed. I make my mother cry even more. The whole room wails with me, our song of mourning. May comes over and hugs me. We yell together. The poet's elegy approaches slowly, methodically.

We hear heavy feet, almost in step, a defeated army retreating, returning home. My mother cries louder.

The poet leads the men into our house. I see my uncles, my cousins, my in-laws. All weep openly as they surround the coffin. My mother calls to the men. The poet sings. The men touch the coffin. The women wail. Minutes seem like an eternity. Time stands still, but not still enough. The poet leads the men back out. Zouzou looks at me as he leaves. We both cry hysterically.

The poet sings from the oaks. The room is in chaos. The women wail. My mother is on her knees before her husband. May squeezes my hand, keeps repeating, "No, no, no." Ghada is tearing at her hair. My aunt beats her chest. "My brother, my brother," she screams at God. Yasmine has her head between her knees, her body shuddering. Sounds abandon my lips, I sweat, every cell in my body grieves, I feel every vein vibrate, every hair follicle alive.

The men come back in. The poet still sings. He calls on God to bless my father. He makes up new verses on the spot, each surprisingly more eloquent. The men wail. Hind rushes up to her husband. They hug and cry together. Zouzou touches my hand. His brother, Akram, stands by us, bawling. My mother screams, "It's not time yet. It's not time. We're not ready." My heart feels as if it is breaking, torn from the roots. A dagger hacks at my insides.

The men walk back out. The poet sings. My mother looks at May. "Make sure they pray," she blubbers. "Make sure it's the traditional prayers."

"They will, Mama," I hear myself saying between sobs. "They will."
    "I'll make sure, Mama," May chimes in.

The men come in. Ghada drops on the coffin, shaking in an epileptic-like fit. Her husband helps her off. May closes her eyes. Yasmine holds my mother. Strident sounds, harsh, overpowering, as my uncles and in-laws lift the coffin. Obstreperous wails echo from the women. My mother screams, "I can't say good-bye." My voice, hoarse. The coffin begins to move. It seems as if all the men are carrying it. My uncle stumbles. The coffin jiggles. More men help as we scream our good-byes. "You make them pray," May shouts at Akram.

The five of us huddle around my mother on the floor. We hug, trying to squeeze ourselves out of pain, confusion, and mystery, out of heart grief. Father has begun his final journey.

"Let's go," May says. "I have to make sure."

Yasmine and Hind stay with my mother. May, Ghada, and I run outside. We hold hands when we are able to see the men. They stand around the coffin, under the canvas, under the secular oaks. It begins to drizzle. The sheikhs stand at the head of the coffin. Everybody has his head down. The sheikhs begin to pray. May starts crying again.

"It's cold," Ghada says. "Let's go in."

"No," I say. "I want to see this. Until they take him away."

"It's too cold," she says. "I don't have my coat."

"I want to see this too," May says. "You can go in if you want. I'll go get the coats."

They leave me standing there. The sheikhs lead the men in prayers. They bless his departing soul. May comes back in her mink, carrying my wool coat and a large umbrella. We watch in silence. When the prayers are done, the older men sit down, and the young men carry the coffin down to the graveyard. "Be careful of your footing," an older man says. The ground is now wet. I see the coffin float down. Beyond it, Beirut, my city, looks asleep. Construction seems to have stopped for some reason. An airplane takes off majestically from the runway. It is so beautiful at times.

May and I walk back to the house, arm in arm, shoulder to shoulder. It is over. Rain slants, falling heavier, thin like wire, like tiny braids of a young girl.

He is buried.

The rain finds cracks in my father's house, in what was once his painting room. My mother considers this the final straw. Yasmine takes her to her room, probably for more tranquilizers. My uncle asks some men to lay a tarp over the crack. He is now the unquestioned head of the family. A new era begins.

I stand in the olive grove, much higher up, where no one can see me. I want to be alone. It has stopped raining. Rivulets and rills surround me, the sounds of moving water. I notice the defrocked poplars. I wonder what they will be like in summer when the sparrows return. I try to imagine. But, nothing. Nothing is in my head. I can't think. I remember from somewhere: the emptiness of mind is better than an absence of soul.

I am upset by a run in my black stockings. They are the only ones I have, my funeral attire. As I begin to take them off, I notice Akram climbing up to the grove. Armed with masculine authority, he approaches, sure of himself. I stuff my stockings in the skirt's pocket.

"I thought I would find you here." His eyes are bloodshot. I assume mine are too. His coat is gorgeous, even though it has ostentatious fur lapels. I always considered him a handsome devil. He is tall, with dark hair, full lips. Even the little gray makes him look more appealing.

"You know it's my hideout."

"Sure do," he says when he reaches me. I blush, embarrassed at my faux pas. I forgot this is where he asked me to marry him. He followed me up here one day when I least expected it. He wanted to talk to me and I told him to leave me alone. He said it was serious. He said he was in love with me. He wanted to spend the rest of his life with me. He proposed in all earnestness. I would make him a good wife. I looked at him and wondered what he saw. He was my cousin, Zouzou's brother. We practically grew up in the same house. Why would I want to marry him? When I turned him down, he asked May. She did not refuse. It was my first refusal. How many have there been? Here I stand, unmarried.

"Are you going to be all right?" I ask him.

His head bows. He begins tearing. The authority melts away, replaced by his never-too-far-from-the-surface boyishness. "I'm supposed to be asking you that," he says. "But, you're the strong one." He begins crying openly. "I'm sorry. I shouldn't be doing this." He looks so defenseless, so vulnerable.

"It's okay," I say. Instinctively, I take him in. I hug him, his face on my shoulders, as I pat his back. He blubbers like a baby. His tears flow easily. I feel a tear drop onto my skin, on my chest. Slowly it dribbles down my breasts, so sensual. Another, then another. I stroke his head. He holds me tighter. A tingle, another tear.

I notice he kisses my neck. I lift my head up to look at the clearing sky, to give him more access. He kisses again, and again. Three times on each area, before he moves on to another. Three times, move, three times, move. Rapacious lips. I smile at the sky. He is no longer crying. His hands are inside my coat, delicately feeling, moving slowly. I shudder, about to laugh. His hand feels my sex. So quick. "Allah Akbar," escapes his lips when his hand finds its plum, its desideratum. His head bowed reverentially, he kisses my breasts through the shirt, paying homage it seems. I wonder why men are so silly. He dexterously pulls my panties down. He wants in. He wants to consummate. I see him unzipping. His penis is unexceptional. He smiles at me. "I have wanted to do this for so long," he tells me. He pushes in, entering violently. It hurts me. He just wants to get it over with, it seems. One, two, three, he is done.

Is this what it is all about?

"I'm sorry," he says. "I have wanted to do you so much, I couldn't control myself." I nod. "Next time will be better, I swear," he says.

He pulls his penis out. It is bloody. "What?" He is shocked. I lift my skirt up. A little blood, less than I expected. "Oh, my God. You're a virgin." All I can do is nod. I also wink at him. "I thought Zouzou was fucking you," he says. I shake my head. I just want him out of there. "Oh, my God. I didn't know." He takes out his handkerchief and wipes his penis. He notices a couple of drops on his fly. He panics. He tucks his penis away and wipes his fly frantically. The blood does not come off. "What will I do?" I hear him asking. "It won't come off."

I take my kerchief, my funeral headgear, and wipe my blood off. I look at the square, white muslin with blood on it. I hold it up. This is better than any painting. It is almost perfect. Stunned, it gives me ideas. My panties and bloodied kerchief join the stockings in my pocket. I regret not having my mislaid handbag.

I walk down the hill, the vindictive wind in my face. Rain falls. I stand outside my father's house. Heavy ropes of clear rain. Noise fills the air, the slash of rain. I am drenched. I take off my coat. Windows shudder. My soul echoes. Gray is the color of rain.

I look down on the streets. Debris floats atop brown and gray rivers. Tar, strips of old and newly paved roads break free and flow along. Stalled cars honk their horns, playing a new melody.

My shirt is soaked. My nipples show. I touch them.

Grace

I would have preferred a car, but my graduation present was a week's stay at a sanatorium in Karlovy Vary. I could not fathom why my parents thought I would need, or even enjoy, such a gift. Both of them were experienced travelers, whereas I was not. They had been going to Karlovy Vary for the past three years. They would leave for a week or two, come back having lost a couple of kilograms and imaginary wrinkles. They enjoyed themselves there, which I attributed to their boredom. They were tired of London, Paris, and Rome. Before Karlovy Vary, they had tried Marrakech and Agadir for a spell. Once, they took me on a trip to Morocco with them, where I was bored stiff. It was a nice country, but there was nothing to do. They, on the other hand, found it fascinating. They thought Czechoslovakia, which was a Communist country at the time, even more intriguing. For some reason, being behind the Iron Curtain held an allure.

It was just my luck. I always thought I was born too late. I was the youngest of four, but with fourteen years difference between my next brother and me. All of my brothers got to know Paris inside and out, and I got stuck with Marrakech and Karlovy Vary.

I want to state here unequivocally that I did not need to lose weight. I might not have been in the best shape, but my health was excellent. I was eighteen. Why would I need a health spa?

The depressing news arrived a month before the exams through the person of my brother Elias. Lina and I were kissing in the den when he walked in wearing his *robe de chambre*. He clicked on the television and shared the couch with us. He treated our kissing as something unimportant that he could easily interrupt for something more worthwhile, such as his watching television.

"So," he said in his agonizingly condescending voice, "I hear you will soon be drinking a lot of water in Karlovy Vary." Elias, thirty-four years old going on twelve, was still unmarried, with no relief in sight. He had been engaged three times, but every girl wised up at the last minute. I kept my fingers crossed, hoping he would find some desperate girl to take him so he would leave the house. He started looking for a wife too late. Even though every girl I knew complained that no good men were left in Lebanon because most of them had gone abroad to avoid the war, he could not find anyone who would take him. He never ever had a girlfriend. Not really. I wondered for a while whether he was a homosexual or something, but he was not. He was stupid and ugly and I was stuck with him in the house. If truth be told, what girl would want someone whose major accomplishment in life was being able to imitate perfectly the sound of an airplane taking off or landing? He grew up wanting to be a pilot, but when he was sixteen, he found out he needed glasses. So his dream ended, shot down, to use a flying metaphor. Pilots were supposed to need perfect eyesight, although I had seen pilots with glasses, so I was not sure if the perfect eyesight thing was true. Anyway, he had to settle for being an attorney like my dad and my other brothers and me in a couple of years. Elias did not like being an attorney. Everyone knew that. He spent all his time on his CB with the signal tuned to airport towers, listening to air traffic controllers and pilots negotiate takeoffs and landings. He knew the name of every Middle East Airlines pilot, even those on loan to other airlines because of the war. He was obsessed, strange, and stupid.

"What do you mean?" I asked Elias. By that time, Lina and I

had disentangled. She hated him as much as I did. She told me he always looked at her as if she were a piece of meat. She was sure he wanted to watch us having sex because he was not getting any. I could understand his finding her attractive and all that, but he truly had no sense of propriety.

He told me that my parents had booked me a week at the sanatorium and had already bought the airline ticket. They wanted to surprise me. I kept calm because I did not want to give him the satisfaction of knowing I was upset. Lina and I left him and went to my room. I was furious. I had expected something better. Lina, who was calm and always tried to see the good in everything, thought it might turn out to be great because I would get all these massages and Czechoslovakia was supposed to be beautiful and all. Still, I was really disappointed. She did think it was terrible of Elias to bring it up that way, so to punish him, we had sex and she screamed and moaned loudly so he would hear and get upset.

Lina had been my girlfriend for three years. She was pretty and her body was just great. Everybody thought we made a great couple and we did, although that was not the only reason she was my girlfriend. I loved her and she loved me. She understood me perfectly. We were in the same class and we got almost the same grades on everything. She had brown eyes like Sophia Loren, although unfortunately not the same bust, but Lina's bust was nice anyway. And her nipples were the best: tiny, brown nubs that were exquisitely erotic. I had never seen anything like them. But enough about her breasts. Her hair was black and smooth. When I first met her, she had short hair, but I asked her to grow it long and she did. I like long hair. I do find some girls with short hair attractive, but they are not as much fun to have sex with, I think. She was Armenian, but both of her parents were born here, so you could not tell that she was not Lebanese.

Lina and I and six other friends went up to Fakra to hole up for a month of studying for the baccalaureate exams. We stayed at the ski house of one of the guys. Pia, our Filipino maid, cooked and cleaned for us the whole time. The schedule was hectic. We would get up at eight and have breakfast. By nine we would start studying till one-thirty, lunch, and then we would study until five. We had a break from five to six, then studied till nine, when we had dinner and then studied until one or two in the morning. It was crazy, but we had a lot of material to memorize. Studying with Lina worked well. Since there was no way we could study everything well, we figured out a system that worked for us. We had sex between five and six every day, which broke up the routine. It kept us sane while the others were going crazy. We also had Lina's sister's notes from the year before.

We sat for the exams. By the second day, I knew I was going to pass. The third day confirmed it. When I was done, my mother told me my surprise. I was leaving for Czechoslovakia the following day.

To leave the country I had two options. I could cross by sea to Limassol in southern Cyprus, about six hours by boat, and take a flight from there, or drive across the green line to the Beirut Airport, which could take anywhere from half an hour to all day. Since it was July of 1988 and there was a lull in the fighting, my parents bought the ticket from Beirut. I was to fly on Czech Air from Beirut to Prague.

Pierre, my father's driver, drove me. We crossed at the Franciscaine, one of the few open roads between East and West Beirut. I was always tense when I crossed. Intellectually, I knew it was the same city. The green line was named such only because it was always green on maps. Nonetheless, whenever we reached the Syrians on the other side and presented the papers, I got nervous. We were from Bikfaya. The president was my father's second cousin and we had the same last name. The Syrians did not like us. But things were calm then and they let us through.

At the airport, I had to show my passport to no less than ten different people before I got to the gate. Ten different times. About half were Syrian. Only one of them was actually passport control. Pictures of Hafiz al-Assad were all over the place. I did not see any picture of our president, Amin Gemayel. I was glad I did not live in West Beirut.

The flight to Prague was terrible. The stewardesses were all fat, which did not augur well for my having fun in a Communist country. The food was terrible. The plane was full of lower-class Lebanese being ordered about by ugly Czech women. How could it get worse? It did. When we landed in Prague, one guy stood up while the plane was still taxiing to get his bag from the overhead compartment. Others were about to stand up when one of the stewardesses, more masculine than most men, came running through the aisle like a television wrestler and pushed the standing man. He fell on his seatmate. The stewardess screamed at him in Czech, berating him for not following instructions given to him in languages he probably did not understand. Let me say that Communism did not make a good first impression.

I took a taxi from the Prague airport to Karlovy Vary. It was quite a distance, but everything was so incredibly inexpensive. The taxi was some Russian model driven by a young man who kept looking sideways at me, obviously trying to engage me in some conversation.

"You like Czechoslovakia?" he asked in accented English.

"Yes," I replied, pointing to the beautiful countryside. "It's a beautiful country." I was not exactly lying. I had never been to any part of Europe before. The greenery was different, warmer, more yellowish. The scenery seemed a lot more sophisticated than back home.

"It is not beautiful," he said angrily.

"It's green." There I was, in a foreign, Communist country, in a car with a mad driver. What if he was more than just angry, but truly mad, as in crazy, insane? Who would ask about me if he wanted to harm me? I had visions of being shot and dumped in some forest, my carcass never to be found. Why was he angry?

"It is not beautiful. People are not happy. No one is happy. It is not beautiful if people are not happy. It is not beautiful. People want to leave. My cousin is in New York. He is happy. He make money. He is happy. New York is beautiful. Here, it is not beautiful."

"Okay." I did not want to have an argument with any unhappy man whether he was a Communist or an anticommunist. Politics bored me. I kept quiet for the rest of the trip.

The hotel was pleasant. I had a room with everything included, full board they called it, and it cost only five dollars a day. It would have been more had I paid in Czech korunas. My parents had a deal with the manager. I had a letter for him with American dollars inside. That paid for the room for my entire stay. I began to see why my parents liked it here. They could live like kings without spending a lot of money.

As part of the sanatorium plan, I had to visit a doctor. My parents told me the visit and the diagnosis were inconsequential. The doctor would tell me which hot spring I was supposed to drink from, how many and what kind of massages, and what kind of mud baths, and so on. No matter what the prescription was, though, I could walk to any masseur or attendant and give him a dollar and get whatever I wanted. It was a good deal. The locals might have to follow the prescribed treatment, but with tips, I could arrange my own. Of course, the doctor found nothing wrong with me. She said I was in perfect health. She told me I should drink twice a day from spring number eight, which on the map looked like the farthest spring from my hotel. She said I could use the exercise. She gave me tickets for two regular massages, one water massage, one mud bath, and one hot-mineral-spring bath. She also gave me a pass to the pool. A boy my age, she said, should swim every day. She put all the tickets in a small plastic holder, which looked just like the ones in which we put our Lebanese ID cards.

It was beautiful country. I took a walk carrying my drinking glass, a slim, ceramic, kettlelike thing. The town was wonderful, but the people were depressing. They walked head down, wearing variations of gray, probably a reflection of their sour dispositions. They missed out on the trees, mostly beeches I think. They also missed out on the river, the Ohře, and the ducks, which were just regular ducks, but I thought they were cute. Then I saw her. She was walking down the hill at a brisk pace, as I walked up. She was unlike anybody I had ever seen. She wore a blue sweater and a bright orange scarf. Her long blond hair caught my eye. She must have been around twenty-five. She noticed me staring openmouthed at her. She smiled, winked at me, and kept walking. She was voluptuous.

Holy Roman Emperor Charles IV discovered the springs in 1347, which is why the city is named after him. I preferred the name Carlsbad. People came from around the world because the springs were purported to heal many ailments, particularly gastrointestinal problems and arthritis. The springs had so many minerals, I wondered how it was possible not to have more intestinal problems. The water was heavy and came out anywhere from warm to piping hot depending on which spring you used. The hotel lobby was a veritable United Nations, except there were no Orientals or blacks. But there were Europeans, Australians, Americans, and Arabs.

I sat close to a group of Europeans, avoiding the Arabs. There were two West Germans, one Frenchwoman, and one Englishman. Their conversation was boring. All they could talk about was the exchange rate, the official and the black-market. Apparently the Frenchwoman was gypped. A young man had approached her and given her an unbelievable rate. She believed him. She gave him five thousand francs. He gave her back what looked like a lot of korunas, but was only money at the ends with cut newspapers in between. By the time she figured it out, the young man was long gone. She could not report it because what she had done was illegal. The other Europeans were all sympathetic. Personally, I could not feel sorry for her. What she had done was stupid. If a Czech could run this kind of scam on her, a Lebanese would probably have stolen her underwear as well.

On the other side of the lobby was a group of Arabs. Three men in their white robes, *dshadeesh* as we called them, sat with their wives, who were dressed in Western clothing. That meant they were not Saudi, but probably from one of the Gulf States. Their children were with the Indian nannies. An overweight boy of about fourteen or fifteen hovered around them. I thought he belonged to them until he spoke. He was Lebanese, a Beiruti. An odd couple, a quiet man in his late twenties and an older, fat, kerchiefed woman, sat on the side. He was unassuming. She, on the other hand, seemed like a paradox. She looked poor, her blouse and skirt seemingly put together with safety pins, yet she wore enough jewelry to dazzle a blind man. I could not place her. She called the fat boy over to her and he came running.

"Your name?" she asked loudly. She was from Beirut, a Muslim, Sunni, probably from Burj-al-Barajneh. You can tell so much from an accent.

"Muhammad." Even when standing, the boy's blubber wobbled. He needed to lose weight.

"Do you speak English?"

"Yes, of course I do." Muhammad looked taken aback that she would even ask the question.

"Good. You have to do something for me." She raised her hand and screamed loudly, "Hey," while waving her hand at the reception desk. The desk clerk came running. "Tell him I have no air-conditioning in my room," she told Muhammad. "How can I sleep in my room if there is no air-conditioning?"

Muhammad translated. The clerk told him he would send someone to fix it as soon as possible. She dismissed the clerk with a wave of her hand. She was so nouveau riche.

I saw the gorgeous woman again in the hotel's nightclub, the only nocturnal entertainment in the town. A live band played terribly. They would have been considered an embarrassment in Beirut, or West Beirut even, and that is saying something. I sat at the bar and watched her. She was with one of the Germans. They were talking and laughing. So she must have been German herself. I noticed his hand touch her butt while she continued laughing. A little later his hand was under her skirt. I could not see why she would let him do that. He was ugly, in his forties, obviously rich. They stood up and left together. She was probably a damned prostitute.

The next day, I walked over to the building where they had the massages. I did what my father told me to do. I put five dollars in the ticket holder. My father said I should give a big tip the first day, which would make them like me. The masseur came up. He said something to me in Czech. I told him in English that I did not speak Czech. His eyes lit up. He looked inside the ticket holder and noticed the five-dollar bill. "Come," he said. "Come." He took me inside. He gave me a towel and pointed to the lockers. I figured what he wanted, but I could not get him to understand that the lockers had no locks. The more I tried to explain the more confusing it got.

He finally gave up, touching my shoulder as if to calm me, and left. I followed him after I undressed. The floor was wet.

The masseur came up to me. He was wearing only wet soccer shorts. He was tall and very hairy, with a black beard as well as lots and lots of chest hair. He did not look Czech. "Water massage?" he asked me. I did not know what that was, so I nodded. Why not? He led me through a corridor. I heard the sounds of rushing water. When we arrived at the destination, I saw the quiet man who was with the Burj-al-Barajneh woman. He was completely naked, standing with his back to a wall, eyes completely shut. Two men stood about three meters away from him in wet shorts. One of them held a hose. He directed the gushing water at the naked Lebanese. It looked painful. The second man's job seemed to be only to give directions. He would scream, the Lebanese man would open his eyes, and the second man would give directions by modeling. He would lift his arms, the Lebanese man would lift his, and the hose man would hit sensitive flesh under arms. This was not what I had in mind when I agreed to a water massage. I kept looking at the Lebanese man's large penis, jumping up and down on its own, wondering if the water is ever directed to that area. My testicles twinged at the mere thought.

My masseur led me to the wall, directing me to face it. I stood staring at the wall, anticipating, waiting for the water. He shouted something, so I held my ground. The water blast was amazing, so strong, it was like a legion of fingers were marching up and down my back. It was slightly warmer than room temperature. He started on my back, my spine to be exact. I felt the water move around. Like magic, I began to relax. I felt flab vibrating. He made the blast stronger and I felt freer. He hit my buttocks and I was in heaven; my legs, then back up to my neck. He kept going for what seemed like an eternity. The water hit the wall next to me. I heard him shout. I looked back. He gestured for me to turn around. He began the process again. This time I could see what was happening. When he hit my chest, my nipples seemed to have a life of their own, shaking to a rhythm all their own.

When the water massage was done, he led me to a stone table. It looked like an altar, carved directly out of the ground. I was supposed to lie on it. What followed was a massage with soap and water. I called it a massage, but it really was closer to a beating. I expected to be black-and-blue by the time he was done. The worst was when he "worked" on my stomach. He would pinch all the extra meat. I began to understand why they were known for gastrointestinal problems. A water massage would cure any constipation problem. As painful as it was, I found myself nodding when my masseur asked, "Tomorrow?"

I left walking on air. The feeling was hard to describe. I was free. I felt unchained, if only for a little while. No one could tell me what to do. I could get whatever I wanted. My parents were not with me. My brothers and the rest of the family were not with me. I was my own man on my own. It felt great.

Walking back up to the spring, I saw her coming down again. She looked even more beautiful. She smiled again at me. My heart leapt. I wanted to follow, but my feet did not obey. She would not want anything to do with me. I drank the spring water and tried to think of Lina.

"You're Lebanese, aren't you?" The Lebanese woman came up and plopped her full weight on the sofa next to mine. I had been able to avoid her for a total of forty-eight hours. Her constant daytime companion, the quiet man, followed suit and sat next to her.

"Yes," I said, "I am Lebanese."

"I am Fatima al-Hajj, and this is Fouad, my driver." She pointed at her companion offhandedly. She put her hand out to shake my hand. I shook her hand and realized the ring with the big bauble had a smaller jewel on the inside, a double-sided ring. This woman was a joke. She had no idea how one was supposed to behave, dress, or anything. "I am the mother of Najib al-Hajj. I'm sure you have heard of him."

"No, I have not. I'm sorry."

I noticed Fouad close his eyes in some form of despair. I assumed he had heard her routine numerous times. My friends and I call this kind of conversation butt sniffing. You know how when dogs first meet, they start sniffing each other's butt. Mrs. al-Hajj was trying to show me how important she was and trying to figure if I was more important than she was. Butt sniffing.

"You haven't heard of Najib al-Hajj?" she asked, appearing slightly perturbed. "You live in Beirut, don't you?"

"East Beirut."

"Ah, no wonder. My son owns Casino du Cheval. It's the most important casino in Beirut. You probably haven't heard of it because you don't cross much. But you must read the papers, don't you? He advertises in all the papers."

"I have never heard of the casino. Sorry." I always wondered why people who could not pronounce French correctly always gave their businesses French names. I could just imagine the kind of casino her son owned. When the war started and the Casino du Liban closed, gangsters with enough muscle opened their own casinos, mostly in West Beirut because it was so lawless. Owners could be divided into two groups. The first were the religious and militia leaders. The second were criminals who had to bribe the first group. Since I had not heard of her son, he belonged to the second, a common criminal who had made it big.

"You have not introduced yourself. What is your name?"

I paused for a couple of seconds for the full impact. "Paul Gemayel," I said as I stood up. I watched her face register. "I have to leave," I lied. "It was nice meeting you." I walked off. Let her sit on that.

Lina called that night right after dinner. I told her how much I missed her. She asked me if I was enjoying myself. I had to admit that I was. The mud baths were wonderfully relaxing. I did not have much to do when I was not getting massages and baths, but on the whole, I was having a great time. She asked me if the girls were pretty. I told her all the Czech girls I saw were ugly.

I was proved wrong. That night at the disco I saw many beautiful Czech girls. It was like a convention. The night before, the club was completely empty. That night, all the girls came out of nowhere. They were dancing with every foreigner in the club. The minute I sat at the bar, a gorgeous blond girl approached me. She had on a ton of makeup. I got an erection just thinking how beautiful she would look if I took her makeup and her clothes off. She stood close to me and in broken English asked me if I wanted to dance. I told her I did not know how to dance, but I would buy her a drink. She ordered a glass of champagne, Veuve Clicquot. I was not stupid. I was not some country bumpkin. I figured I was being had. I asked her how much. For ten dollars, I could have my way with her for an hour. We left for my room.

I was back in the nightclub, content, within ninety minutes. She was on the dance floor, trying to hook another client. I noticed Fouad sitting at a table with seven girls and another man, who looked Lebanese and appeared to be translating. The table had bottles of champagne, wine, and Scotch. I felt ambivalent about helping Fouad, yet I noticed myself walking in his direction.

I bent and whispered in his ear, "They're prostitutes. They want you to spend money on them because they get a cut from the bar. You don't have to. You can take one up to your room for only ten dollars."

"Thank you for telling me that," he said kindly. He was very soft-spoken. "I know they're prostitutes." I left him and went back to the bar. He remained at the table for thirty minutes, talking to the girls through the interpreter. After that he stood up and walked off with a girl much more beautiful than the one I had had sex with. Lucky dog. He winked at me as he passed by. I hoped he did not think we were now friends.

While floating in hot mud, completely covered except for my head, I heard two Englishmen talking in the next room.

"It's those bloody Arabs," one said.

"Why?" replied the second.

"They tip so much. Before they started coming, you could get the royal treatment dirt cheap, but the Arabs are so stupid, they throw money away. They have ruined it for all of us. Everyone now expects at least a dollar tip."

The al-Hajj woman settled her girth on the chair next to mine. I brought down my *Herald Tribune* in acknowledgment, then went back to reading, hoping she would get the hint. She did not. Fouad was next to her.

"I need to ask you a big favor," she said. "I need your help."

"What can I do for you?" I tried being completely polite.

"I would like to buy chandeliers. These people here are known for their chandeliers."

"They are?"

"They sure are and they're terribly cheap."

"And what has that got to do with me?"

"We have to go to Prague to buy them. Neither one of us speaks English. You can. You can come with us and translate."

"You want me to come with you to Prague so you can buy chandeliers?" I asked incredulously.

"Yes," she said, completely oblivious to my sarcasm. "We can get to know each other on the way. We have to take a taxi in the morning. We'll just drive to Prague, buy the chandeliers, and come back, maybe have lunch on the way."

"Why me?"

"Because you speak English."

"Ask someone else. I am busy. I have three massages tomorrow morning. I can't go to Prague and miss them."

Surprised, she first looked at Fouad and then at me. "But I need you," she said in a whiny tone she assumed was persuasive.

"You don't need me. You need someone to translate. You can find someone else, I'm sure."

"There is no one else," she insisted.

"What about the man from last night?" I asked Fouad. "He should be able to do it much better than I could. He spoke Czech."

Fouad was trying to shake his head discreetly. His eyebrows were moving on their own, and his eyes pleaded with me not to mention anything more.

"What man?" Fatima asked.

"No one, no one," I said to Fouad's relief. "Why don't you ask Muhammad? He speaks English and I'm sure he wouldn't mind a drive to Prague."

"Muhammad? The fat boy? You expect me to go to Prague with a fat boy? Maybe you didn't understand me. I will be buying chandeliers. I can't go with the fat boy."

"Why not?"

"Because he doesn't have class. You do. You're from a good family and you speak English very well. You should come with me."

"I can't go. I have massages." I stood up and left. I could not understand what the stupid woman was talking about, and I no longer cared to find out. I walked away without looking back.

———

That evening, I told Lina all about the crazy al-Hajj woman. She could not understand her either. We talked for a while. She asked me again about the girls of Czechoslovakia. I told her I had still not seen a beautiful one. I hoped I sounded convincing. I was thinking of the German woman.

The club was not as full as the night before. Fouad sat next to me at the bar. He bought me a drink.

"Thank you for not saying anything to Sitt Fatima about last night," he said sheepishly.

"Do you work for her?"

"For the time being. I work for her son. I'm one of the drivers, among other things. Her son didn't want to send her alone, so I had to come along. She is a good woman. A little crazy, but a good woman. She does want you to come with her tomorrow. It would help a great deal if you did."

"Why? Why me? She can take the fat boy."

"She doesn't want him. She wants you. If you don't come with us, then she'll be in a terrible mood, and I'll get the brunt of it. I know I'm asking too much, but it won't take long. Only a couple of hours. It will help me a great deal."

"I don't know. I don't see why I should go."

"There's no reason you should go. She just decided she would like that. Now she has her mind set on it. If you don't come, my day will be completely miserable."

He looked so depressed telling me all this, I was unsure what to say. I kept shaking my head, hoping everything would go away. This man and I had nothing in common. He was a workingman, poor, uneducated. We would probably never have talked if we were not Lebanese in a foreign country. Yet, here we were, sitting facing each other sideways at the bar, his eyes like a puppy's at a pet store.

"Okay, okay," I heard myself saying. "I'll come. But it's only for a couple of hours. We'll go to Prague, buy the damn chandeliers, and drive back."

"Yes, that's all." He was smiling now. His whole demeanor changed. The al-Hajj woman must be a complete bitch when she did not get what she wanted. "You're a good man, a good man. If there's anything I could do for you, just let me know."

There was nothing, of course, that he could do for me. I hoped never to see those two again, once I left. Actually, he was not a bad sort. She was the one I would never want to see again.

The German woman came in. I could not keep my eyes off her. She was dressed all in black, not her usual collage of colors. She sat at the other end of the bar, ordered a drink, and kept looking at us.

"So who was the man last night?" I asked my drinking mate. "Why can't he go with you?"

"He's a student here, going to school on a Hariri scholarship."

"Why can't he go with you then?"

"Because my boss doesn't want his mother to meet him."

"How come?"

"Because he works for him. The boss doesn't want his mother to know anything about his operations."

"Works for him? Here? How could he work for him? I thought he owned a casino or something like that."

"He does. And he uses a lot of Czech girls, if you know what I mean?"

"As prostitutes?"

"Yes. They come on six-month assignments. They're very popular with the customers."

I was flabbergasted. Not by the fact that Fouad was a pimp, although that was shocking enough. Not by the fact that a casino in Beirut was a brothel, there were lots of brothels in Beirut. I was shocked that any girl would come to Beirut to become a prostitute while a war was going on. It never ceased to amaze me that Filipino and Sri Lankan girls came to a war-torn country to work as maids, or more accurately pseudo-slaves. Their countries were so poor anything was an improvement. But this was Europe. As bad as Czechoslovakia was, it was still better than Beirut.

"How many girls?" I asked.

"About twenty every six months. We get a lot of applications. They make a lot of money. They come back here and live like rich people."

"That's really unbelievable. And I thought I was warning you last night."

He laughed. "I appreciated that. Really, I did. All the girls at the table are coming to Beirut in three weeks. That's why I was meeting them."

The German woman was openly staring at us. I looked at her, wondering what to do. As I thought of buying her a drink, she stood up and walked over to us.

"Hello," she said. She asked Fouad in German-accented English if he would like to dance with her. My heart sank slowly. I told her Fouad did not speak English. Her smile got wider. "Dance?" she asked him. He knew what that meant. Both of them, completely ignoring me, walked to the dance floor. They slow-danced to a fast song. Their hips were joined. Within less than a minute, no one could mistake where the dance was leading. By the time the song ended, they kissed. By the time the second song ended, he was leading her to his room, winking as he passed. I could have killed him, I was so envious. Why not me?

The road to Prague was a straight line. That was how I remembered it. It may not have been, but the roads were wider than anything back home, so it looked as if we were traveling in a straight line. Unhappily traveling, if you asked me. I sat in front next to the taxi driver, the crazy woman and the betraying gangster in the back. I did not speak to the driver. I did not want another political diatribe. We got into the taxi and the crazy woman had no idea where to go. She assumed that Prague was one big store selling chandeliers. She told me to tell the driver she wanted chandeliers. I had no idea what to do. Finally, Fouad said we should just go to Prague. We were bound to find something.

And the German picked him over me.

"Are you going to go to university?" the al-Hajj woman asked me.

"I don't know." I did not want to engage her in any conversation. I was intentionally rude, hoping she would take the hint.

Ten minutes later came, "Do you come to West Beirut?"

"No."

Which was followed a little later by, "You should come and visit the casino sometime. You would be a special guest. Everybody enjoys himself there. You would have fun."

"I'll think about it."

She kept trying till we reached Prague. We entered the city. Its beauty entranced me. The buildings, the bridges, all conspired to lift my mood momentarily. All of a sudden, the crazy woman screamed in English, "Here, here, here," pointing frantically to a store across the street. Lo and behold, there stood a lighting store, with chandeliers showing through the large windows. She became frantic when the driver could not turn right away because of the embankment. He had to go to the end of the street, turn on the *rond-point,* and return. She practically tore her hair out.

By the time the driver had parked the car, she was already in the store. Fouad was smiling, as if sharing a joke with me at her behavior, but I did not smile back. I wanted to get this over. The al-Hajj woman did not need my services. She walked in and two salesgirls appeared at her side. She pointed and they gave orders. Within ten minutes, she had everybody in the store working for her.

The boys carried the packed chandeliers, the girls smiling and writing down orders. She came out with eleven chandeliers and I did not have to say a word. I was furious. She did not ask for prices. She did not ask anything. She pointed at the ugliest, most ostentatious chandeliers, and they got them for her. I walked outside for some needed fresh air. Fouad followed me.

He lit a cigarette and offered me one. I did not take it. Even if I smoked, I would not have taken it. "She didn't need me," I blurted out. "I don't know why I came on this stupid trip."

"I know. I'm sorry."

"This is so stupid," I fumed.

"Yes, it is. But I am grateful. I appreciate your coming. It means a lot to me." Fouad was leaning on the car, smoking, looking calm. I would have been calm too if I had made love to the German the night before.

"I just want to get back," I sighed. "I want this over with."

"We will soon be on our way." He looked at me, so completely understanding, I felt even more uncomfortable.

It did not take long to load eleven crates into the taxi. Four went into the trunk, which did not close, but was tied with a string. Seven crates were then tied to the rack on the car's roof.

Shopping must have induced a different state in the al-Hajj woman. She became even more talkative. She talked to herself, but I was not listening. She wanted to buy me lunch and I declined.

"How about a soda? Are you thirsty?"

"No."

"Well, I want one." She ignored me and spoke directly to the taxi driver. "Drink. Pepsi." The driver understood. He stopped at a small store in the middle of nowhere, a brick building, which looked completely out of place.

"You are very ungrateful," the al-Hajj woman told me angrily before she opened the door and got out.

I was shocked. "Ungrateful?" I asked too late, because she had already slammed the door. "Me, ungrateful?" I got out of the car to run after her and scream in her face. I was so angry. She had already gone into the building. Fouad caught up to me from behind halfway to my destination. He held me, his arms enveloping me completely. He calmly told me to relax. She did not mean what she said. She was crazy. Slowly, I felt myself melting in his arms. I calmed down, but he refused to release me.

I stood on an empty road, between Prague and Karlovy Vary, in front of a lonely building, being hugged by a gangster, with a Czech taxi driver staring at me, thinking I was crazy.

The years sailed on, rough seas, harsh winds. Time has been unkind to us. Ungracious winds damaged our sails. Elias initiated the precipitous descent. He killed himself that week while I stood unsullied before the water hoses. He departed our oppressive world without a farewell note, but was found by my father with a model Middle East Airlines plane in one hand, a gun in the other, and a bullet in his head. It shook my mother to the core. What followed caused her to wear ill health as a favorite coat to protect against the unfeeling weather.

At first, I thought my grief was for my mother, not Elias. At the funeral, she was totally unhinged. In fact, she never truly recovered. It was later, much later, that tears flowed for Elias. After I cried for my father, for my mother, I realized how sad Elias's life was, how unfulfilled.

I arrived home from Prague and was met by the driver, who would leave us shortly thereafter, wearing mourning black. Child that I was at the time, my first thought was how inconsiderate of Elias to kill himself and ruin my homecoming. I was a fool. As sad as the funeral was, little did any of us know that it would be the last time the whole family would be together.

The summer of 1989. The president of Lebanon's seven-year term ended. Amin Gemayel left for Paris apparently packing suitcases of government money. Our family suffered the consequences. Our monies dried up. Rene Moawad got elected president and assassinated in the same month. Elias Hrawi followed him, but General Michel Aoun considered himself the true president. The ubiquitous war erupted again, only this time brother slaughtered brother literally. General Aoun lit up the skies. Samir Gea'gea', the head of the Lebanese Forces, discovered the lost art of pyromancy. We killed each other while the Syrians watched on the sidelines, cracking open dried watermelon seeds. They watched East Beirut in flames, waiting for the self-inflicted massacres to cease in order to eradicate the fools who were left standing. They succeeded.

My father was killed in the first purge, not long after Elias killed himself. An unknown assassin murdered him while he was driving home. As luck would have it, he was not driving home from work. He had none at the time. No one would use his services for we had become an outcast family. He was actually driving home after attempting unsuccessfully to broker a political dispute between my two older brothers. How anybody figured out where he would be driving remained a mystery. No one was at my father's funeral. It was considered unwise to attend. Even my gladiatorial brothers missed it. I stood there alone with my mother wondering how we could have ended so out of favor.

My mother's black wardrobe was sufficient since she only had to wear it for one more somber year. She was bedridden in January of 1990 and never left her bed after. She died in August of that year. Her funeral was better attended than my father's, but less than Elias's. I had become an expert on funerals, a necrologist. I grew up quickly.

By the time the dust settled, my family was broke, completely out of the power loop. I was still at university, but I had no discernible future.

I found a job when I graduated, a real job, where I actually had to work, as opposed to the vaporous job I would have gotten had our family fortunes fared better. I was a legal assistant at a large firm. I worked for an attorney whose family owned the entire firm. There were three assistants. We did all the work while he pontificated over Turkish coffee. He reaped the rewards.

Lina suggested we see other people. I could not blame her. I loved her, but I was no longer a "fun" person, as she put it. I was mired in a deep depression and could not seem to pull myself out of it. She thought it would be better if I went out with someone else. I wanted to object but I could not. I wanted to offer her hope, but I never had it.

She was married, eight months after what she called a timeout in our relationship, to Pierre Ballout, eight years older than I and a thousand times richer. I did not even merit a wedding invitation.

I cried for Elias some more and wondered if I should follow him. For the longest time I could not see the point of going on. As time passed, I realized that I grieved for Elias more than I grieved for my parents. What he represented for me, I was never sure. Maybe it was that he ended his life. Maybe it was that he had never found out what it was about. I did not know. I did know that, for a long time, I considered ending my life every morning, and decided, every morning, that I would not do it that day. That I would go on for one more day. For one more chance.

———

Years pass and one adjusts. I live by myself in a small apartment in West Beirut. It is terribly small, but with a lot of character. I know, I know. Everything terrible has character, but it is true in this case. I painted it all lemon yellow with a carmine trim. Gaudy colors, but with a lot of *character*. You would probably wear sunglasses coming into my place. It's great. I do have a view, you know. An incredible view, believe it or not, from my living room and the balcony. The balcony can't even take a single chair, but three people can stand and watch the sun set into the Mediterranean. Every evening I get treated to a wondrous miracle. I have not missed a single sunset, not one, since I moved into my place. Every day at dusk, I am thankful.

Today is my twenty-sixth birthday. Hear this. It's a surprise party, but I am cooking. Can you believe this? Here's how it goes. My friends wanted to surprise me with a birthday party. In all, it would be about twenty-six people. My apartment can fit twenty-six people. We have done it before. We sit on each other's lap. In any case, my friends could not afford to both buy me presents and cater the party. It was an either/or. None of them could really cook for twenty-six, or at least not cook well enough for a good party. I am the best cook. Samira, bright girl that she is, decides to solve the problem by telling me to cook for my surprise party and pretend to be surprised. What the hell!

Samira and her husband, Makram, take me out to a movie. The gang waits at my apartment until we return. Wow. Surprise. A party for me? Let me check on the lasagna. Look, I have enough paper plates from the last time! Now, isn't that a true miracle? I don't think anybody bought it, but the party goes on whether I am surprised or not!

The party starts at ten. By midnight I am pleasantly tipsy, while everyone around me is rip-roaring drunk. As usual, someone jokes about the excess smoke in the room. Another person makes the customary reply that the smoke ameliorates the colors of the room. The usual jokes about my bad taste are thrown only to be lobbed right back with pointers on style, with an emphasis on their lack of it.

Through the haze I notice her. She is sitting on my friend Kameel's lap, but they are obviously not an item. She smokes, and in profile she looks exactly like one of those Marlene Dietrich pictures, same color hair, same cut, same nose, curves and straight lines in a divine combination. She is nothing short of delectable. He says something to her that I cannot make out. She giggles, and I am entranced from across the room. She laughs gently, charmingly at first, before following it up with a full belly laugh. She did not grow up here for few Lebanese women allow themselves a full-fledged belly laugh. *Elle se sent bien dans sa peau.* Kameel notices me staring, and they both start crawling in my direction. He does it because he is drunk, he even sways as he crawls, and she seems to find it amusing to crawl. I notice more lines, more curves. Her blue dress has a strategic, tear-shaped water stain on the left cheek of her rump, which sways seductively, forcing me to fall deeper and deeper. She arrives slowly, her blond bob appearing first, begins to look up at me, her hands on my thigh for balance, and gently lifts herself up. "Happy birthday, Paul," she says in accented English, a familiar accent. What can I say? My heart flutters, my dick draws blood from the rest of my body, my mouth drops, and my tongue dries up. She sits on my lap. Kameel sits on my other thigh. It will only be a matter of time before he crashes on the floor. Sooner than later, I hope.

"My name is Helena."

"What part of Czechoslovakia are you from?" I ask.

"How did you know?" She seems slightly puzzled. Her blue eyes twinkle enough to entrap me. I am completely enchanted. "Did someone tell you?"

"No, I recognize the accent. I spent a week in Czechoslovakia in 1988, but it left am impression."

"In 1988?" Helena talks too fast, shaking her head as she speaks. I find it charming of course. "That was so long ago. There is no more Czechoslovakia. Now it is the Czech Republic. It has changed so much."

"I can imagine."

"Prague has changed so much. You would not recognize it. It is completely different. It's like a stone has been lifted off the people. Everything changed so much. You must come visit again. It's so different. People are happy."

"Only if you come with me," I say, squeezing her gently. "I'll go anywhere with you."

"I know where you want to go with me." She giggles. I think we are going to get along really fine. I like her. "I live here now. I only go back to Prague at Christmas."

I hesitate before asking, but I finally do. She is not a prostitute, or as she put it, not a practicing prostitute. She arrived here in Beirut, fulfilled her contract to none other than Najib al-Hajj of the now defunct Casino du Cheval. Al-Hajj was killed when the war was over. The one and only Fouad opened a bar and restaurant where Czech girls hung out. Apparently it is doing well. Helena, my charming Helena, is managing that joint, not just the prostitutes as she hastily points out, but the whole thing.

She insists we call Fouad. She must tell him she has met me, who knows him from so long ago. It's two in the morning, but she is sure he is still up of course. We're in the kitchen, the quietest room right now. She dials Fouad's number as I sing "Falling in Love Again" in a hoarse voice to her. She doesn't get it. I lower my voice even more and belt out in a terrible German accent, "I can't help it." She still doesn't get it. Fouad asks to speak to me. He is sweet. We exchange pleasantries, but then he asks me how I am doing. I tell him it's my birthday and I am doing great. We must get together he says. Can I have lunch tomorrow? Sure I can. I can have lunch. Overhearing, Helena coos, "Late lunch, okay?" Late lunch it is, I tell Fouad with a smile. Do I need anything—a job, money, anything? No. No. I don't need anything. I am quite happy with what I have in my hands. Helena giggles. Fouad laughs. Do I need a chandelier? He laughs. He can get his hands on a number if I want one. My turn to laugh. We say good-bye. "Need anything?" Helena asks me in broken Lebanese. "Hmm." I smile pruriently. "I might need you to love me." She kisses me deeply in the kitchen. We sit on the counter and I try to teach her the words to "Falling in Love Again," but she can't stop laughing.

Fatima al-Hajj showed up at the church uninvited. To be more precise, neither Helena nor I invited her. Fouad did. Since the wedding was small, attended only by friends, Fouad could not resist her insistence at showing up. I was glad she did. Fouad found me before the ceremony started and apologized, saying he still could not say no to Sitt Fatima.

She looked out of place at the wedding, but in a good way. Her son was killed during the war and his fortune squandered. Fouad supported her. She seemed to have reverted to her natural state: no jewelry, no ostentation, just a regular, old, somewhat-on-the-plump-side Beiruti woman. She was still talkative. She did not stop talking to whoever was sitting next to her during the whole ceremony. She was still obnoxious in her own way. After slobbering Helena and me with kisses, she actually pinched both my cheeks, telling anybody who would listen to her that I had been her friend for years. She slapped Helena's behind and told her to make sure she gave me a couple of boys. Helena, not understanding a word she said, slapped Fatima's behind right back, laughing. Fatima was still the same, but somehow changed.

Fatima took me aside, saying I needed some motherly advice. She wanted to know why I did not want to leave my apartment for a bigger one. I was making money now. Fouad wanted to give me the apartment and I should take it. Didn't I want to live in a good place? I was married now. I needed to move up in the world. I explained to her that both my wife and I loved our apartment. We had been living there for a year. It was small, but we both really loved it. Fatima kept on insisting that we needed a bigger place. She went round and round until she finally burst out with, "Well, my gift might not fit in your apartment." I could not stop laughing. She soon joined me, but in between gasps she made sure to tell me that, no, it was not a chandelier. But we could not stop laughing anyway.

A Flight to Paris

It is said that one must always maintain one's connection to the past and yet ceaselessly pull away from it. The former I did not believe in, the latter I followed religiously. I had no use for memory. If left unburied, it festers, like an untreated wound. I was never able to deal with my past. Some mechanism must have been turned off within me while I was growing up.

I would not say I ran away. I called it moving on, always looking forward, on the go, astir, engaging life fully, never dwelling on what I could not change.

At times, I was unsuccessful. It crept up on me.

Was I avoiding loneliness? Most definitely. I had lost most of the people I held dear in my life. I lost the love of my life, Tom, two years ago. After twenty-two years of not being apart for more than forty-eight hours, how could I not be lonely without him? Did I miss him? More than anything I could think of. Did I think of him? Not a day went by without my thinking of him. Did I dwell on it? No. It was too painful. I moved on. I looked forward. I went on with my life.

Did I cry for him? I wished I did. I came close a couple of times in the beginning. Tears welled up in my eyes, but then my head would suck them back in. Dry like the Sahara, my head desiccated the tears, a phenomenon, to be sure.

———

I figure I have six months. I am not sure whether to enjoy them, knowing everything I have tried to avoid is going to fall apart, or try to prepare everybody for something they do not really want to face. Shall I begin causing slow pain now or spare them for the six months and hit them suddenly? The question I ask myself is whether the duration of pain or its prodigality is the more agonizing.

The Air France flight was not full. I had my customary aisle seat. I took off my shoes, took out my book, and made myself comfortable. An attractive woman sat in the window seat. The seat between us was empty. She smiled pleasantly as I sat down, then went back to searching her handbag for something. I was glad. She looked like someone who could keep her own company. The flight was long, at least ten hours, and nothing was worse than sitting next to someone who filled the air with palaver for fear of being in her own company.

She looked foreign, probably Mediterranean, most likely Italian, Roman. Fair to dark skin, brown hair heavily highlighted with blond. The dye job alone must have cost a small fortune. She wore some designer suit. I never followed fashion, but there was no doubt she did. She was obviously well-off. Her makeup was impeccable if you went for that sort of thing. You knew she had it on, but it was not overpowering. She was probably my age, around forty-five, unless her best friend was an incredible plastic surgeon.

For whatever reason, I found her somewhat offensive. I could not believe someone would go to all that trouble to present herself in such a fashion. I preferred uncontrived presentations, a more natural look.

I have the window seat. I prefer it because I can think by windows. They close the plane door and no one is in the middle seat. The man on the aisle seat is terribly handsome. He must be a homosexual. I bet my son knows him. I am sure they all know each other. Maybe they have had sex. No. Stop it. Stop it. I cannot keep doing this.

How could he do this to me? How could he? After all these years, it is as if he were a completely different person. Well, he is. He is a different person. He is a man now and I love him. Even if that damn boy will not listen to a word I say, I still love him. I should have killed him, but I love him.

I hope they burn his goddamn book.

Where did I put those damn nicotine gums? I must find them or I am in deep, deep doo-doo.

My seatmate must work out. I can tell even under his dull shirt. Probably spends a lot of time at the gym, just like my son. How can they go to all that trouble just to build up a few muscles? Anyway, I prefer a more natural look.

Paris. The city of light. The city of memories. Who would have thought I would be back there two years after his death? Tom did. He planned it. He wanted his ashes scattered all over Paris. I thought of ignoring his wishes. After all, he was dead.

I could not.

Nostalgia. Paris is the city of nostalgia. What did Yourcenar call nostalgia, the melancholy residue of desire? What was left of my desire?

It was in Paris that I met Tom. We fell in love in the Pasteur metro station of all places. Two fags from the City by the Bay had to come to the City of Light to fall in love. After moving in together, we started coming back to Paris every year for Valentine's. I had not been there in three years.

They are going to have a field day when the book comes out. In six months, all the bitches will be abuzz. Samira, the grande dame of tattlers, is going to have a ball. She breathes scandal. She sucks it in with clean air and exhales matter more bilious. She can slander anybody with even a whiff of a rumor. What will she do with this, a book detailing his sexual exploits as a young boy in war-torn Beirut?

Why did he have to do that? Detailing everything so graphically, a sex toy for all the militiamen. Why? Why would he reveal something so people would revile him?

Where is that damn gum?

There they are.

"There they are," she said, taking out a package of some sort. She looked at me sheepishly. I figured she must not have realized she said it out loud.

"My nicotine gum," she said by way of explanation, holding the package up. "It's a long flight and they are making it harder and harder for us. I really need the gum."

While she was busy looking all over the place for her trove, she had missed the announcement that Air France had a special standing section for smokers. Between first class and economy, elites and proles, was the smoking section where smokers could fulfill their vice and the rest of us would be spared because of curtains. Recycled air was not yet a consideration for Air France.

I wondered if I should have told her. I settled for leaving her with a smile, or what Brad, one of my few remaining friends, described as more of a ghastly leer. I was out of practice with smiling.

He's the silent, handsome type. Like my son, I guess. He is probably making fun of me as does my son as well. I should hide my Ludlum book. I bet he is reading some pretentious literary book. Oh, dear, Thomas Mann. He is worse than my son.

Desire. Whatever happened to my concupiscence, as Tom used to call it? I had not gone out with anybody since he died, which meant I had not had sex in over seven years. By the time he began to get sick, he no longer wanted to have sex. He no longer wanted to share beds. We stayed intimate, but our desires were interred in sepulchres deep within, never to raise their troubling heads in the time we had left together.

Brad thought I was not going out with anybody because I had not gotten over Tom yet. That was only partly true. The main reason was that I didn't know who would even want to go out with me. I looked around me. I saw all kinds of attractive men. I looked at myself and wondered what had happened. How did I get to be this ugly? I tried to convince myself someone would want me because of my personality, because of my mind, or whatever. But did I really believe it? No. No amount of positive visualization, no amount of mantras repeated, could change that fact. *I* would not go to bed with me. It was that simple.

I was older. I was forty-five years old. At one time, I might have been acceptable, but not now. Let me put it this way. I was never comfortable trying to find a man to have sex with when I was twenty. How could I be now, old, decrepit, and plagued with a pernicious virus? After twenty-two years with Tom, I have been violently thrown back into the lion's den, only to find that no lion wanted to eat me.

I will spend a week in Paris before going on to Beirut. I need to recuperate. Shop, shop, shop. I need my retail therapy.

When the no smoking sign went out, and the addicts ran to the front, she figured it out. She looked puzzled for a second, then looked at me and said, "I didn't know they allowed smoking."

"They have a special section up front," I said. "They announced it earlier."

"Oh, silly me, I did not hear them. I bet they announced it in English or French and I missed both. I never pay attention. That's what my son always says. I never listen to him."

Why not? Mann refused to overwhelm me, sleep was certainly

not an option, and the mere thought of a French film with the ubiquitous Depardieu was stultifying.

"Your son?" I asked. That was all it usually took.

"Oh, yes. My son lives in San Francisco."

- My son lives in San Francisco now. He came to go to school here when the war started and never came back. That's the war in Lebanon. We're Lebanese. And I don't mean he never came back to visit because he did that a lot. He never came back to live. He could not adjust to Lebanon after living here. He broke our hearts. It was a big mistake sending him here, I think. And so does my husband.

- A mistake?

- Yes, a big mistake really. He is alone here. No one to take care of him. He lives with someone, but believe me he is alone. I don't care how long they have lived together. He's alone. He has no family behind him. I mean we're behind him most of the time, but he's too far away. He wants to make his own life, he says. Why? What's wrong with the one he has? That's what I say. His father is going nuts. He's our only son. And now we know he's not going to get married. No grandkids from him.

- He lives with a man?

- Oh, yes. He's gay. I don't want you to think I'm homophobic. I'm not. You can sleep with whomever you want. But do you have to be blatant about it? I told him. I told him the first time he told me he was gay. I said it's okay. Lots of people are. Lots of great people. They don't advertise it. You can get married, have a nice family, and do whatever you want discreetly. Of course, he doesn't listen to me. Not only does he live a gay lifestyle, as he calls it, but he writes a book. He wants the whole world to know.

- He wrote a book?
- Yes, he wrote a novel. I read it. They tell him it's literature. I think it's trash. It's all sex. He has sex with everyone. He has sex with the entire male population of Lebanon before the age of fifteen. Why is that literature? It's just a porno book. You know, like *Emmanuelle*. Why would he want to publish a book like that?
- He had a lot of sex before he was fifteen?
- Oh, no. That was all made up. I know my son. When he was young, he was straight. Maybe he had ideas, but he didn't have sex with men till he came here. He made it all up. Some of the things he said in the book could not possibly have happened. He was in bed every night by nine, for crying out loud. I know my son. The only thing that turned him on was reading a book.
- Fascinating.
- It's very confusing. I don't know why he would do such a thing. Everyone is going to think these things actually happened. They will think not only is he a homosexual, but he's a whore too. He will have no one to support him. No one.
- But he has a lover.

She refused to acknowledge her son's relationship. I tried different angles, but she parried expertly. She relented at one point by admitting her son has been living with his roommate for eight years. In her mind, her son was gay, but he did not have sex. Her son was gay, but he did not love. It was only a concept.

Tom meant the whole world to me. For twenty-two years we were one entity. Even our names were perfect, Tom and Jerry. One could not say one name without the other.

Our parents, unlike this woman, did not even want to acknowledge our existence, let alone our relationship. We ended up being an independent couple when it came to our relationship with the world, and a dependent one when it came to our relationship with each other. We rarely went out or had friends over. We spent our evenings together. We went on holidays together. Few people were ever a part of our life.

He was sick for six years. I was the primary caregiver, which was harrowing. When he died, I was left completely alone. Alone, in a manner that I had never expected. My peers at work were extremely sympathetic. People I knew called to offer advice. Life went on, but I was not living it. I worked at all hours to alleviate feelings I wished would remain buried. Life went on, but I was a mere observer.

Ever since Tom had died, I felt I was sitting in a bus, alone, looking out a travel-stained window onto a world of people rejoicing, dancing. The bus I rode on was going in a different direction.

- Why do you think I am insulting you?
- I did not mean you are insulting me. I said your dismissal of your son's relationship so easily is insulting. Let me ask you, do you love your husband?
- Of course, I do. I love him very much. We have been married for thirty-eight years.
- Thirty-eight? That can't be. You don't look a day over forty-five.
- You're so nice. You guys are such good flatterers. I should have you around me all the time. I've had a good surgeon do my face.
- Wow. Well, anyway, why do you think your love for your husband is different from your son's love for his lover?
- I don't know. It just is. I don't mean to be prejudiced, because I try hard not to be. Deep down, I know it is. Maybe I

am prejudiced. I can't see how they love each other anyway like I love my husband. Okay. I'll admit that my son loves him. I'll admit that. But, it's different.

- How do you think it is different?
- We're . . . I was going to say we're married, but I know that they would get married if they could. He keeps telling me that. I see your point, but it's still different. It is just different. I can't explain.
- Do you think humans can choose who they love? Did you choose to love your husband?
- What a question. I'm not sure I can answer that. Let me think for a minute. I don't know whether humans can choose who they love. I don't think I had any choice. I loved my husband the first time I looked at him. He was such a handsome young man. So gallant. I have never looked at another man. I could not conceive of loving another man. You're smiling. Did I say something funny? This is the first time you smiled. Are you laughing at me?
- No, not laughing at you. Do you think your son can choose who he loves? Don't you think he loved his lover the first time he looked at him too? Do you think he could conceive of loving another man? Don't you think that sometimes he goes to bed at night and is terror-stricken wondering what would happen to his life if his lover dies? Don't you think he loves him so much, his heart hurts, it really hurts?
- I don't know. How would you know he does? You don't know him. But we're not talking about him, are we? God, I sound like a therapist. You're smiling again. You're either finding the gin or me amusing.
- The gin. Blame the gin.
- Are you in a relationship?
- No, I am not.

- Really? I would have sworn you are. You sounded so in love. So romantic. So wonderful.
- No, I am not. I need to stretch my legs.

Why did I do it? She revealed her secrets. I was not going to.

Tom used to call flight encounters "airplane friendships." You met someone, you revealed things you would never tell a close friend, let alone a stranger. Then you never saw them again. Instant intimacy. The Chinese food of relationships: you were satisfied quickly and an hour later you were hungry.

I was not hungry.

He looks at me in a funny way, halfway nonchalant and halfway as if carrying the weight of the world. Then he blurted it out, just like that. It took me by surprise.

"My lover died of AIDS."

- Oh, dear. I am so sorry. When?
- Two years ago.
- Oh, Blessed Mary. That's so sad. How long were you two together?
- Twenty-two years.
- Oh, my God. I don't know what to say. Twenty-two years is a long time. You must have loved him so much. I am so sorry. It must still hurt you terribly.
- I'm fine. I try to keep going.

She cried. I was so envious. My lover died and she cried. I wished I could ease her pain. I wished I knew what to say. How could I tell her that her disaster is such a minor event? Who really cares if a book is published these days? Everybody would figure out her son is gay. Was that such a big deal? Did that compare to a life of loneliness? Was that as big a tragedy as a life that could never again be partnered? How could I move on if no one wanted me? Who was I kidding?

- I don't know if I would be able to handle something like that.
- It got a little crazy. He developed fungal meningitis in his brain. They could do nothing about it since it grew on the outside of the brain, but inside of the skull. No blood can reach there so we couldn't use drugs. It gave him migraines. The fungus could not push out of his cranium, so it started pushing out right over his left eye. This thing seemed about to explode out of him. You know, like *Alien*.
- That's awful.
- We were referred to a head surgeon. I remember her so well. I'll probably never forget her name, Afifa Labban.
- Really? That's a Lebanese name. She's probably Lebanese.
- She was such an awful woman. I still get angry just thinking about her. To this day I am angry.
- It also could be an Egyptian name. Yes, she's probably Egyptian.
- She told us she could get rid of the fungus. Her solution was very simple supposedly. She described it to us in graphic detail. First she would cut the skin below his forehead and pull it back to get to the cranium. Then she would saw out the front part of the cranium and take it out. She would then pull the brain out and dust it off, remove all the fungus.
- What? What do you mean pull out the brain?
- That's what she said. She would pull it out a little to get to all the nooks and crannies.
- You're smiling. You're pulling my leg.
- No, I'm not. That's what she wanted to do.
- That's crazy. Was she going to use a Dustbuster?

- Spring cleaning. But the crazier part was we considered it. It's not just that. When she finished cleaning it, she would put back the front part of the cranium and staple it in.
- Staple it?
- Yes. Staple it. She was going to staple the cranium and sew his face back on. Or maybe the top of his head. I can't remember where she wanted to do the cut.
- And you considered that?
- Yes. For about fifteen minutes. I was desperate. Tom was in shock at first. But then all of a sudden he said to me, "Do you remember when we talked about how we were not going to do anything extreme to save my life? Do you remember? I wonder if this isn't a little extreme?" Then he started laughing. The surgeon came into the room to find us hysterically laughing. We couldn't stop.
- He must have been such a courageous man.
- He was.

I do not know what to say to him. I don't know how to translate our words of condolence into English. Would it have mattered to him anyway? He must be in such pain. I don't think he wants to talk anymore. I will leave him alone. Maybe my damn son would have been able to help him more than I can. Damn him. Damn him and damn that fucking book.

In a darkened plane, somewhere over Greenland, as the passengers watched Depardieu save the entire French film industry, I cried.

Remembering Nasser

While reading, I was reminded of a walk I used to take when I was much younger, during the summers in my father's hometown. Memories of Nasser kept interrupting any attempt at concentration, so I put the book down. We run from the house before anybody can stop us for chores, through the back, behind the fig trees, which provide us with good cover, and over the back fence to the back road. To the family cemetery, my family's not his, for he will be buried, is buried now as a matter of fact, in Barouk, his father's hometown, which was higher up, farther west, than my father's. I am alive, but he is dead. Who would have bet on that outcome? I feel the stone in my hand as I read, sitting on my sofa, in my house in San Francisco, the sharpness of it, the weight, as I throw it at the gravestone, lapidary phrases seared in my mind like sentences in my book. My cousin Nasser, on one of those walks, stands atop a stone and reads, "Sheikh Nadim Talhouk, 1903–1957," as he counts how many years that makes. "I can beat that," he says proudly. He did not. Like a basketball announcer who tells us how well a player shoots his free throws right before the player misses, Nasser jinxed himself. On the walk, that day, he took his penis out and peed on Sheikh Nadim, desecrating what I once thought to be sacred, urine cleansing the old stone, making circles, my eyes fixed, aghast. Seductive blasphemy.

My mother saved pictures of all her children in photo albums, each organized with dates and descriptions. Almost half of all my pictures in the albums included Nasser. There is a series of four pictures dated March 1961. I was eighteen months old, he was twenty-two months. A professional child photographer must have taken them, for most of the photos look terribly contrived. We sit close to each other, shoulder to shoulder, and look at a small basket. I put various toys in the basket. He waits for me to finish, after which he takes the basket and stands up. The last picture shows me trying to get up, to follow him most probably, his diapered butt framed in the picture as he leaves.

I recall a poker game at Ann Arbor. It must have been 1978 or 1979. Nasser was visiting from England where he was attending some pay-for-a-degree college. The game was in my apartment. I was in my room, out for a couple of rounds, trying to reacquaint myself with my lungs after a heavy bout of cigarette-induced coughing. The whole table was Lebanese, as most of my acquaintances were at the time. This was long before I came out. Nasser felt at home. Someone made a joke I did not hear. I heard Nasser's voice though. "No, no, no. I'll not have it. Don't make fun of him while I'm around. I'm his cousin."

Fred, my lover, was jealous of him. It completely confused me. Fred used to say my face would light up whenever I spoke of Nasser. If he called, I would run to the phone. He was like my twin brother. How Fred could be jealous was beyond me. Sometimes I wonder whether I should have blamed Fred for what happened. What difference does it make? He is dead now too.

A classical pianist who was once a student in our school came back one day to talk to each class about piano playing. He then tested separately each boy and girl. When it was my turn, he had me turn my back to the piano and played a note, then a second note. I had to tell him whether the second note was lower or higher than the first. I got them all right. I knew I was doing well because he stayed longer with me than with any of the others. With Nasser, the test only lasted about half a minute. The pianist tested me for at least five minutes.

At the end of class, he wanted me to deliver a note to my parents. In it he told my parents that I was talented and I should be given piano lessons. Nobody else in class got a note. I gave the note to my mom when I got home. She waited till after dinner to tell my father. I was sitting in the den, playing with Nasser quietly, which we were supposed to do when my father was home. We heard my mother tell my father that I should be taking piano lessons. We heard my father say that he did not think it was a good idea. He thought I was too effeminate as it was without piano lessons. I felt Nasser move closer to me. He did not say anything. We sat next to each other and played with the Matchbox cars in front of us.

A phone conversation:
>—I have to get married.
>—Why?
>—What do you mean why? It's what I want. People get married.
>—I know that. I meant why now?
>—Because it's time. I'm tired of being a bachelor.
>—Why all of a sudden?
>—I don't know. I don't have matching plates.
>—What are you talking about?
>—I have no idea. Issam slept over at my house while he was here, and then when he went back to Beirut, he told my mom I don't have matching plates. I don't even know what

matching plates have to do with anything. Mother called and said I needed a wife because I don't have matching plates.

—You're getting married because your mother wants you to have matching plates?

—Fuck you. I need a wife. What's wrong with that? I want someone to greet me when I come home. I want sex. I'm tired of looking for it. We don't all live in America where everybody fucks like rabbits.

—I thought you were fucking that woman I met.

—She's married. I can only fuck her when her husband is not there. I need something more permanent.

—So you want to get married?

—That's what I said. Why are you making a big deal out of this? I want to get married. We're all going to get married. Why not now? It makes sense. I'm not a young buck anymore. Neither are you, you fucker. You should start thinking about getting married. It'll make your father happy. You should be happy for me. I tell you I want to get married. You should be happy. What kind of friend are you?

—Hey, I'm happy. If you're happy, I'm happy. I only wanted to know why now. Who's the unlucky girl?

—Fuck you. The *lucky* girl. She'll be damn lucky. I don't know yet. We're looking.

One of my earliest memories is of an occurrence in a bathroom. I do not know where, or in what house. It is evening. Nasser and I are in the bathroom with a maid. She must be Egyptian or Lebanese because the language is Arabic. The tub is full. We are supposed to take our nightly bath, but we are using the toilet. Both of us need to shit. Nasser sits at the commode for a while. I feel really uncomfortable. I tell the maid that I need to go. She tells Nasser to get up and let me have a go. He complains that he is not done, but gets up anyway. He turns around to plead his case and I see a small, greenish-colored turd in his anus. I tell him he can go back to the commode and finish. I can wait.

I must have been no more than three.

In 1976, before either one of us left for school, during a lull in the fighting, we were in Chouiefat, driving towards Beirut. Nasser was driving his father's car without his father knowing. Whenever his father had a card game, Nasser stole the car for a couple of hours and we took turns driving. A well-dressed man waved at us to stop. He asked us nicely if he could ride with us to Beirut since he was in a hurry. He sat in the back behind Nasser. He was charming as he conversed with us. He treated us like adults. As we drove, we noticed a new checkpoint on the road. Nasser started cursing. He hoped nobody would recognize him and tell his father. I thought maybe they would figure we had no license. Our passenger calmly told us not to worry. It was not us they were after. He looked distracted. At the checkpoint, a man in civilian clothes with a big handgun put his head in the window. He smiled at us. He said something about the danger of picking up strangers. The man then bent Nasser's head with his left hand and with the other shot our passenger until the bullets ran out. Blood spurted everywhere. Our passenger died with a smile on his face, as if looking forward to death. It was the closest I would get to see firsthand the new breed of Lebanese fighters, those who would dedicate themselves to the ultimate sacrifice. I sat with my back to the window, facing the man with the gun, mouth agape. He let go of Nasser's head.

"You never saw what I look like, right?" he asked us. He sneered. "I don't want you young boys getting into any kind of trouble. Do we understand each other?"

Nasser could not even look at him. He was staring straight ahead. He could not bring himself to move.

"Do we understand each other?" the man repeated more sternly.

Nasser still could not move. He seemed paralyzed. "We didn't see anything," I screamed in a high-pitched voice. "We didn't see nothing."

"That's good. Now why don't you drive home."

Nasser still stared ahead, unable to move a muscle. The man wanted us out of there, but Nasser could not move. Finally, I struck the back of Nasser's head with my hand. "Move," I screamed as loudly as I could. Finally, he looked at me. "Drive," I yelled again. He put his foot to the pedal and we were out of there.

We drove for less than a kilometer. When we got to Khalde, I told Nasser to stop at the side of the road. I got him out of the car and walked him over to the beach. I dragged him into the water, both of us fully clothed. I washed him, washed the blood off. He let me dunk his head in the water to untangle the blood. I washed him, punctiliously and ritualistically, like washing the dead, or a blood baptism, the color intensifying in the water surrounding us and then dissipating quickly. I tried to remove as much of the blood as possible.

Once done, I took his hand and he followed. I walked him home, hand in hand, all the way. We left the car. It took us an hour and a half to get to his house. He was still unable to say anything and I did not talk to him, just walked him home. By the time we arrived our clothes were dry. We looked haggard, but that was not unnatural for us. Nobody noticed the remaining bloodstains. I undressed him and threw the clothes out. No reminders were left.

We did not say anything to anybody. The car was found with the corpse of a man who had betrayed a militia leader. Everybody knew which handyman had killed him, but nobody would have been able to touch him in any case. It was assumed the car was stolen to kidnap the man and kill him.

We were free.

We never ever spoke of it.

Another early recollection. Nasser and I shared a room, as well as a bed, in the mountain house, when we were younger. Through our window, when we first arrived, we always saw a blanket of red. The poppies covered the sloping field. Nasser and I would look through the window trying to find the one, lonesome poppy that was not part of the larger blanket. There was always one, sometimes two, rarely three, independent poppies, not like the rest, different. We loved that poppy.

Years later, I was reminded of that poppy while reading. Proust saw it too. He called it the poppy that had strayed and been lost by its fellows. As I read that, the memories came flooding back.

I met Fred in grad school. More precisely, I met Fred while I was attending Stanford and he was there to give a speech on the economies of the Middle East. I was in his hotel room within an hour of the end of his speech. I surprised myself. I was still closeted, but allowed myself to be seduced. He came on so strong that not one of my classmates had any doubt as to what was happening. He asked me to leave with him while everyone was still around. He outed me, so to speak.

We were together until he died in 1993, eleven years, only seven of them healthy, though.

I can be walking when all of a sudden something reminds me of him. It can be anything, a flower, a man wearing a pair of jeans in a certain way. If I see a painting, I think of McEnroe, who is now an art dealer, which would of course bring me back to Nasser.

I remember him as he was when he was young, without the mustache, the fat, the alcoholism; fourteen, fifteen maybe.

Brother,

My hand trembles so I cannot write. I cannot face you either because I will do harm. I am furious. How could you do this to me? I will leave you two . . .

The note was crumpled and thrown in the wastebasket. He said he did not want me to see it, but he left it in an empty wastebasket.

He could not stay in an apartment with my lover and me. Fred was furious. Nasser was furious. They both blamed me.

From the beginning, Fred had wanted me to come out to my family. He thought as long as I did not tell my family about our relationship, I was not really committed to it. I could not. I was out in the United States and closeted in Lebanon. My two lives were separate. I felt it was better for everybody that way. When I met Fred, I cut out anything in my life that was Lebanese. Lebanon became this place I visited twice a year. To this day, I have not told my family.

When Nasser had to come to the United States for a business meeting, he thought he should come and stay with me for a week in San Francisco. I tried to clean up, to remove any trace of gayness in the house. Fred was livid. He did not allow me to move anything. My clothes and I were to remain in our room. Nothing would be hidden. He thought Nasser, if he loved me as much as I thought he did, would accept the situation. I told Fred there was no way Nasser would accept the situation. Once he knew, all he would be able to see when he looked at me was someone who takes it up the ass. Fred said there was more to being gay than taking it up the ass. Not for Nasser.

In the beginning it was Ilie Nastase, the great Rumanian. Nasser idolized him. We played tennis constantly. I do not think either one of us could ever have been a great player. We were not athletically gifted, nor were we ever truly coached. Later, Nasser dropped poor Ilie for John. No one was more Nasser's alter ego than McEnroe. I loved Borg, but Nasser breathed McEnroe. To Nasser, he represented everything that was great about the world.

I remember I was at Nasser's house visiting. Fred was sick back in San Francisco, but I needed a break. Nadia was making breakfast. Nasser's two-year-old, Layla, came in from the kitchen laughing loudly. "Abed is here," she kept repeating. "Abed is here."

Nasser picked her up and swung her around. "Don't embarrass me in front of your uncle," he chastised her jokingly.

"Who's Abed?" I asked.

"The driver," he said. "She has an infatuation for our driver."

"Layla, you little tramp!" I joked.

He looked at me funny.

Nasser's father, Habib, was the family clown. Everybody loved him because he made you laugh, everybody except Nasser. I remember Nasser once telling me, after he had a few drinks, "How can you respect a man who left absolutely nothing but debts for his wife and children?" He truly abhorred his father, which I did not realize while Habib was alive, but which became apparent after his death. My father paid for everything when it came to his sister and her boys. They lacked nothing. Nasser began to idolize my father. It was only gradually that I realized I was being replaced.

After college, Nasser went to work in Kuwait through contacts that my father provided, while I stayed in the United States. First I stayed because of grad school, and then it was a great job with Booz·Allen, a management-consulting firm. At one point my company wanted to transfer me to Saudi Arabia thinking that, as an Arab, I would be able to handle things better than the last couple of executives, who had burned out. I refused. They dangled money, status, and all they could think of, but I did not budge. I was starting a family in San Francisco with Fred. My father could not understand my wanting to stay away. At first, he conceded it was not a bad idea because the war was dragging on, but still he wanted me closer. Europe would have been preferable for him. I did not wish to tell him that the East Coast was too close to Lebanon for my taste. It was not that I disliked my family. I loved them dearly. I wanted a barrier, distance being the best I could think of, between us. I could not see how I could possibly be a complete person, let alone a gay one, if I hung around. Nasser hung around.

Slowly but surely, he became the son my father wished I were. He got married to a nice Druze girl from the mountains. They had a real house with matching plates, and she gave Nasser two boys and a girl. When the war was over, Nasser moved his family back to Beirut. Every time I went back to Beirut, I saw as much of Nasser as I did my family. He spent all of his time with my father.

Nasser picked up my father's mannerisms. He talked like my father. He walked like my father. He gained weight like my father. He combed his hair like my father. He smoked like my father. And he drank like my father.

He died of heart disease and liver problems, exactly like my father.

I never liked confrontation. When I was a young boy, Nasser's mother would always try to get me to fight other children. I never wanted to fight. All the other kids would fight just to please her and other adults. They would constantly wrestle. I could not. My aunt would try to shame me by suggesting that her daughter could beat me. She probably could. She was a tomboy then, and years later, even after a marriage and four kids, I could swear that she was a lesbian. In a different culture, she would have been a true butch dyke, and a happy one at that.

In 1972, Nasser and I started a neighborhood soccer team. We called ourselves The Firebirds, an exotic name. We played a couple of games against other teams. In what would turn out to be our last game with the team, we were playing against another team with an older boy who must have taken offense at the way I looked or something. He wanted me to fight him. He was cussing and harassing me the entire game. At one point, while the game was going on, he started calling me names and stood directly in front of me, face-to-face, not allowing me to go around him. I was unsure what to do. All of a sudden, Nasser came out of nowhere and punched him.

I had to enter the fray. While both teams watched, and no one tried to stop anything, Nasser and I beat up on this guy. I never fooled myself into believing that I added much to the fight. Nasser alone could have taken him out. But I tried to help. I held on to one of the older boy's arms so Nasser could beat him up more easily. When the damage was done, the rest of our team made fun of the way I had fought, limp wrist and all. That only made Nasser more furious, screaming at them for standing around and not doing anything. We stopped playing soccer.

Tennis suited us better.

I dream about Nasser. He is a constant landmark in my dreams. I even have recurring dreams with him in them. In one, Nasser and I, as teenagers again, walk along until we arrive at a fork in the road. We don't know which road to take. Each road has its own enticing features. We decide that he will go right and I left, and then we can tell each other what it was like when we get home.

As a young boy, I would walk alone for hours. I would take a book and read as I walked. I would go out of the house to be by myself. I told myself stories of escape. I fantasized about being somewhere else.

———

One afternoon, in 1974, Nasser's mother was playing cards at a friend's. We skipped school. We had some hash stored up. We ended up in his house, on the sofa, getting wasted. The house reeked, which we thought was totally hilarious.

His father walked in, shocking the hell out of us. "Hi, boys," he said as he went straight to the bathroom. Nasser looked at me, shrugged, and we started giggling. Habib came out and was about to leave again when he looked at his watch.

"Aren't you boys supposed to be in school?" he asked.

"We're home to do a science experiment," Nasser replied.

"That's good. Okay then, I will see you boys later." He turned the door handle and was about to leave when his nose twitched. "What's that smell?"

"Smell?" Nasser asked.

"Must be the oven," I said.

"The oven?"

"Yes," I replied. "The science experiment was in the oven."

"We were trying to dry a bird's nest," Nasser added.

"Except we burned it, which is why it smells."

"It was wet because of the rain."

"So we put it in the oven to dry," I went on.

"But there were no eggs, just the nest."

"And it burned."

"So it wasn't a complete failure because we figured out the combustion point."

Nasser's father just kept nodding. "That's good. I'm glad you boys are so studious. Keep up the good work." And he left.

"Combustion point?" I snickered. We giggled for a couple of hours.

He told no one about Fred. He tried to pretend he did not know and never saw. Nonetheless, the wall went up. It might have seemed to the naked eye that it was the same, but since that day, it never was.

I was there when he proposed to his wife, if you could call it that. Once Nasser decided he was going to get married, his mother began the requisite search. Before Nadia, he had gone out with two girls. He flew to Beirut for both dates. They met all the criteria so he asked them out. I had heard rumors, which he denied, that he was proposing on the first or second date and being rejected. He did not deny the rejection, only that he had asked so early on in the game.

With Nadia, I saw it happen. It was their second date. I felt like a Lebanese meze so I went to a restaurant and they were both there. Nasser could not understand how I would want to be alone in a public place. I had to sit with them. She was pretty. That was the only thing I could be sure of about her. Two hours later, Nasser was talking about the time to get married. He was twenty-eight. She was nineteen. He told her he would be interested in marrying her. She said she had to think about it.

She did look up to the ceiling at one point and whisper to herself, "Nasser and Nadia," and sort of nodded her head.

Years later, when I brought up the overheard conversation about piano lessons, Nasser was shocked that I still remembered, surprised that I still blamed my father. He said I finally left home and if it were important that I take piano lessons, I would have. He said if it were such a big deal, I should take piano lessons now. Wasn't I the free one now?

A conversation at the sickbed:
—You know, Nasser was that way too. He was always grumpy when—

—I know. I know. When you both had mumps, you were put in
the same room and—

—Okay, okay. I get the hint.

—And you looked like matching bookends, with both your necks
so swollen, and they kept you in that room for three weeks—

—I get the picture. I shouldn't have brought it up.

—And you had a wonderful time, both of you, even though
Nasser was grumpy at times, because he's always grumpy
when he's sick.

—I'm sorry. Okay?

In another picture, dated the same in 1961, definitely by the same
photographer, Nasser and I are looking up, something above capti-
vating us, probably some toy. We look longingly.

How old were we then, nine, ten? The cemetery was our favorite
place. Few people went through there, so we had the place to ourselves. Our favorite grave was unsigned. It was built like a small
pyramid with only three layers of marble. We tried to move the top
slab numerous times. It was incredibly heavy. As Nasser got
stronger, the marble slab frustrated him more and more.

Years later, after the war, I got Nasser to come walk with me
through the cemetery. I wanted to see what it looked like. Exploded
shells littered the grounds. The cleanup crews had removed the
mines but not the "litter." Our favorite grave was damaged, large
holes and chips in the marble, yet the slab itself was unmoved.

"How could anybody do this?" I asked rhetorically.

"I did that. One time I got really angry, I came here and shot
the fucker."

I took him by the hand once—we could not have been more than
five or six, maybe seven—and led him to his sister's room. Every-

body was out of the house so it was completely safe, but still he was nervous. I took out all her Barbies.

"You want to play with her dolls?" he asked me.

"Yes, it's fun."

"What if we get caught?"

"No one will know."

"I don't want to play with dolls."

"It's okay. You can be Ken."

There is a word in Lebanese that has no corresponding word in English. *Halash,* or *yihloush*, with a heavy *h,* means to pull hair out, or to yank someone's hair. I always assumed that there was a Lebanese word for it, because we do it often, both to other people and ourselves. All you have to do is attend a funeral and you will see what I mean.

I began to wonder why a word did not exist in English when I saw Nasser pull his newlywed wife's hair and take her to the bedroom. I was visiting them in Kuwait. They had been married for about seven months. It was about nine-thirty at night. Nasser asked if I wanted to get high. I agreed. Nadia had this look of utter disbelief. Nasser went into the bedroom. She followed him. I did not hear what she said, but she seemed perturbed. I heard Nasser say calmly, "What's the big deal?"

Nasser came out with a pipe. He lit it and gave me a hit. We both smoked. Nadia came out of the bedroom, slamming the door, and went into the bathroom, slamming the door. She obviously had not locked the bathroom door because Nasser followed her and dragged her out by her hair into the bedroom. I heard a slap. Nasser came out as if nothing had happened.

"I guess you have not smoked in a while," I said.

"No, it's been a while."

Next day, Nadia was as chipper as ever.

My father grew suddenly old and sad, fast, with full sail. It happened in only a few months. One trip he was fine; the next, six months later, he seemed engulfed in a sea of sorrows, his face sagging, crushed by the burden of idleness. He had stopped working between those two trips.

One time, my father sat in the den, in his chair, with Layla on his lap. He rocked her as she played with his sparse, white hair. She pulled a strand forward towards his eyes. "Ouch, you little devil, you," he said, and tickled her. She giggled and tried to do it again. Nasser crouched next to my father. "Be careful when you do that," he told his daughter. "You don't want to hurt Grandpa." He blew his daughter a kiss, and seemingly unconsciously, he flicked my father's lock of hair back in its place. My father closed his eyes.

I had to return for his funeral two months later.

When Fred started getting sick, he withdrew. I could not get through to him, did not know how to talk to him. I took care of him, but I was unable to be there for him. When he started getting sick, I began to feel lonely again.

Nasser and I used to play phone tricks. We were good at it. One of my all-time favorites is calling some lady and pretending we were phone technicians. Nasser would tell the woman to put her finger in the number four and dial. Then put it in, say, number seven and dial. Finally he would tell her to put her finger in her ass and dial. My other favorite was calling the pharmacies. I would call one and ask the pharmacist if he had a thermometer. He would say yes, and I would tell him to shove it up his ass, then hang up. Then Nasser would call ten minutes later and in all seriousness ask the pharmacist if some kid had called a while back and told him to shove a thermometer up his ass. The pharmacist would say yes in a huff. Nasser would tell him it was time to take it out, then hang up.

When Nasser got married, he began to get rounder till he finally achieved his final pachydermatous heft. The last time I saw him, I realized that somewhere in there was the boy I used to know. My father succeeded in killing himself with excess, but it took him a lot longer than Nasser. My beautiful Nasser was a quicker study. He died at thirty-eight, a couple of years after my father, a couple of years after Fred.

While reading, I was reminded of a walk I took when I was much younger. Nasser and I were in the cemetery. He was being his usual mischievous self. He challenged me to throw stones at different graves. He looked at a grave of a Talhouk. "I don't like any of them," he said. He took his dick out and peed on the grave, on the entire family. "Don't keep your mouth so open," he said, "or I will pee in it." He laughed.

We sat on our favorite grave, the pyramid. He took out his hunting knife. "I have to cut you," he said. I resisted. I did not understand why we would need actual blood. Wouldn't calling ourselves blood brothers be enough? He cut the tips of my two fingers and put them in his mouth. He looked in my eyes the whole time. Shivers ran up my spine. I made small cuts on the tips of his fingers. I put them in my mouth and sucked. He let me suck on his fingers for as long as I wanted.

"We are now brothers," he said.